COMPLICATED
BY:
CHENELL PARKER

PROLOGUE

Rylee sat at her desk, silently willing the clock to switch from four fifteen to five o'clock. The rest of her week flew by, but this particular Friday was dragging on for no apparent reason. Maybe it was because she'd finished her filing earlier than usual, but she was bored out of her mind. Being a legal assistant/paralegal, Rylee stayed busy most of the time. Her boss had been in and out of court for most of day, so she really didn't have much to do. With the amount of business that the law firm had, she knew that it could be a matter of minutes before that changed. She would be so busy some days that she wouldn't make it home until eight or sometimes later.

Deciding that she would play a few games of solitaire to pass the time away, Rylee turned on her computer and waited for it to power up. Although it made her sad most of the time, she couldn't help but to stare at the photo collage of her family as it flashed across her computer screen. Rylee and her sister, Baylee, were the only two kids that their parents had. The pictures on her screen reminded her of the good times. She remembered the times that she and her family visited Hawaii or Jamaica for every summer vacation. The times when deciding what she wanted to wear to a party was the only thing that she had to worry about. A time when she had both her parents and her sister there to talk to whenever she needed to. A time before her oldest sister's estranged husband shot her down in cold blood before turning the gun on himself. The pictures reminded her of how beautiful her mother was before the cancer made her unrecognizable and eventually killed her. Her father's smile was so genuine and not forced, like it had been during the final months of his life. That was, before a massive heart attack eventually killed him and left her all alone in the world.

Although she was happily married to the love of her, Rylee still felt empty inside. At only twenty-one years old, she had seen more heart aches and heart break than most women twice her age. She was thankful for her paternal grandmother and her aunts and cousins on both sides of her family, but it just wasn't the same. Rylee's husband, Mekhi, had a huge family, but even they couldn't fill the void of her deceased loved ones.

"Anybody else scheduled to come in today Rylee?" her boss, Mr. Campbell, asked when he walked through the front doors of the office.

Brian Campbell wasn't just Rylee's boss; he was also her father's best friend up until the day he died. His son, Brent, and Rylee were also close before he moved away for college. Mr. Campbell and Rylee's father, Ryan, graduated law school together and opened the criminal law firm that she was now employed by. Mr. Campbell had an almost flawless record in criminal court and his list of clients was extremely long. He'd since moved his office from Lafayette, Louisiana and relocated to New Orleans. He now had family, criminal, corporate, and employment lawyers on his team as well. Rylee originally wanted to follow in her father and older sister's footsteps and become a lawyer, but she gave up her dream after their deaths. She was making a pretty good salary as a paralegal and she was okay with that.

"I don't think so, but let me double check just to be sure," Rylee answered.

"Okay, but if we don't have any appointments, you can call it a night and start your weekend early," Mr. Campbell said, making Rylee smile.

She hurriedly exited out of her game of cards and pulled up her calendar to make sure she was free to go. Rylee went through the list carefully and exhaled when she saw that she was free and clear for the remainder of the day. Just as she was about to exit out of her computer, the front door chimed, alerting her of an incoming visitor. Rylee immediately plastered a smile on her face when she saw a petite, caramel-colored woman with beautiful eyes walking towards her desk, followed by two other men. Just by looking at the woman, Rylee could tell that she had been crying. She was used to seeing distraught family members come in on a daily basis, so that was nothing new to her. She grabbed a few Kleenex from the box on her desk and handed them to one of her unknown visitors.

"Thank you." The woman smiled weakly while dabbing her eyes with the tissue.

"You're welcome. What can I do for you?" Rylee asked.

"I know that y'all are about to close, but I really need help. I'm trying to hire a lawyer for my brother," she spoke up through her tears.

"Okay, do you have an appointment?" Rylee asked, even though she knew that she didn't. Her name would have been on her calendar if she did.

"No, I don't have an appointment, but I really do need to speak with a lawyer. My brother is going to court soon and we had to fire his old attorney. He's being accused of shooting somebody and they're trying to charge him with attempted murder. His lawyer wasn't fighting hard enough, so I need a better one. I don't care how much it cost; I'm desperate at this point."

Usually, Rylee would have turned her around, but she heard the urgency in the woman's voice. She still had her calendar up on her computer, so she decided to help her out.

"What's your name?" Rylee asked her.

"My name is Zyra Henry and my brother's name is Zyrian, different last name though," she answered.

"Ok Zyra, give me a minute to see what I can do," Rylee said as she added her name to the calendar of appointments.

Zyra stood at her desk as she got up and walked to Mr. Campbell's office. It only took about three minutes, but he agreed to see her once he got off the phone with another client. Rylee was relieved that he agreed to help and so was Zyra. Before returning to her seat, Rylee hurried and locked the door before anyone else could walk in.

"How long has your brother been in jail?" Rylee asked, trying to make small talk.

"He's been in for a year now. I know you hear this a lot, but he really is innocent. He's taking a charge for somebody else and they're trying to throw the book at him,"

Zyra said, looking over at one of the men who accompanied her there.

Rylee never noticed before, but he looked scary. His appearance alone intimidated her, and she turned her head as soon as they made eye contact. Not only was he over six feet tall, but he was all muscle.

"I understand. My daddy was a lawyer and he always told me that just because a person's in jail doesn't mean that they're guilty," Rylee said, repeating one of the many things that her father told her.

"You damn right. My cousin ain't never even been to jail before in his life. He ain't no snitch and that's the only reason he's locked up now!" the man bellowed, making Rylee even more nervous.

"This is my cousin, Grim," Zyra said, laughing at how Rylee was looking at him.

Grim Reaper is more like it, Rylee thought to herself.

"Damn, you fine as hell. You got a man?" the other man asked flirtatiously.

"Boy, sit down!" Zyra yelled. "Don't mind him. That's my other cousin, Buck."

"Yes, Buck, I'm actually married," Rylee said, flashing her ring. "And by the way, my name is Rylee."

"What you mixed with Rylee?" Grim rudely asked, causing Zyra to slap his arm.

"Grim, shut the hell up!" she whispered harshly before apologizing to Rylee.

Rylee only smiled, but she wasn't offended by the question. It wasn't the first and probably wouldn't be the last time she heard it. It was really bad whenever she hung out with her paternal grandmother, cousins, and aunts. People would look at her crazy, but she learned to live with it a long time ago. Even when she showed people pictures, they looked at her sideways like she was lying about something. Rylee's father, Ryan, was white, but she never saw a color when she looked at him and her other family members. They were her family; nothing more, nothing less.

Her mother was black, but that didn't stop her from catching Rylee's father's attention. Her mother, Leela, was a part-time model who met her father while looking for an attorney to look over her modeling contract. From what she was told, it was love at first sight and had been that way up until death parted the two of them. Rylee was a mixture of both of her parents right on down to her name, which was a combination of both of her parents' names.

Rylee and Zyra made small talk and got to know each other for over thirty minutes before Mr. Campbell came out of his office. Just like Rylee, Zyra was married with no kids, but both of her parents were still alive. Her brother, Zyrian, was her only living sibling and Rylee could tell that they were close. Zyra informed her that her older brother was killed in a drive-by shooting a year prior, and Rylee felt her pain, since she too had lost a sibling to gun violence. Rylee busied herself straightening up the office, while Zyra and her cousins talked to Mr. Campbell. It was almost six o'clock when they finally emerged from the office, but Rylee wasn't complaining.

"I'll see you Monday Rylee and I'll be calling you sometime next week once I've gone to see your brother Zyra," Mr. Campbell said, right before he left out of the office.

"Judging by the smile on your face, I'm guessing your meeting went well," Rylee said to Zyra.

"Hell yeah. Aggravated battery sounds a lot better than attempted murder. Since he's never been to jail before, he might not have to do that much time. If they didn't have a witness, he probably wouldn't be doing any time at all," Zyra replied.

"They might not have a witness if I catch up with that nigga," Grim responded seriously.

"Don't start with your bullshit Grim. You've caused enough trouble already," Zyra fussed.

"I knew you just couldn't wait to throw that shit up in my face," he replied angrily.

"But anyway," Zyra said, rolling her eyes at her cousin. "I owe you big for this Rylee. I know that you had to talk up for me in order to be seen and I appreciate that. What do you have planned for this weekend?"

Usually, Rylee would chill with her husband at his sports bar on the weekends or hang with one of her cousins. Zyra seemed cool, so she didn't mind switching up her routine to hang out with her.

"I don't have anything special planned. What did you have in mind?" Rylee asked.

"Let's do dinner and a movie, my treat. I really want to do something nice for you to show my appreciation," Zyra answered.

"That sounds good to me. Let me give you my number and get yours too," Rylee suggested.

She had no idea that from that day forward, she and Zyra would be practically inseparable.

4 years later...
Chapter 1

" Zyra calm down. Everything is already done and the cake will be there in a few hours," Rylee said, trying to ease her friend's nerves.

After five years behind bars, Zyra's brother, Zyrian, was finally being released from prison. He had gone to a halfway house a few months ago, but now he was coming home for good. Since it was early May, Zyra and her family planned a huge picnic and seafood boil in City Park to welcome him home. Rylee helped her best friend as much as she could, but Zyra was still a nervous wreck. She wanted everything to be perfect for her little brother's homecoming. Although Zyrian was a grown man at almost twenty-seven years old, Zyra still considered him her baby. She was only two years older than him at twenty-nine, but that bit of information was irrelevant to her.

"Okay, but are you still coming early like you promised?" Zyra asked.

"Yes, Zyra. I'm looking through my closet now, trying to find me something to wear."

"I don't know why, when you know Mekhi is going to beg you to wear something different. That nigga act like you're a trophy or something," Zyra replied.

"Shut up Zyra," Rylee laughed.

"And please tell me that you booked us at MJ's for his party weekend after next," Zyra rambled on.

She was so excited that Zyrian was being released two weeks before his twenty seventh birthday. He'd spent the last five birthdays in prison, so Zyra wanted to do something special for him. Rylee offered to let her use MJ's to throw him a party, free of charge. Zyra was sure that Mekhi didn't know about that bit of info. He was all about his money and he didn't believe in doing nothing for free.

"Girl, how many times do I have to tell you that everything has been taken care of? I did that months ago, when you found out that he was coming home. Stop stressing yourself out over nothing. I'll see you in a little while," Rylee said before disconnecting the call.

"What's wrong with her crazy, confused ass now?" Mekhi asked from his spot in the bed.

"Shut up and stop calling my friend confused. You gon' slip up and say that shit in front of her one day," Rylee fussed.

"But, she is confused. She'll be with a man today and then swear she's in love with another woman tomorrow. I don't blame her husband for leaving her. He needs to sign the divorce papers and be done with her ass."

"It's his fault that she's the way she is in the first place!" Rylee yelled.

"You always taking up for her crazy ass," Mekhi said, frowning at his wife.

"You damn right I'm taking up for her. Best believe she would do the same thing for me," Rylee snapped before walking out of the room.

Mekhi just shook his head without bothering to reply. If he didn't know anything else about his wife, he knew that she was loyal. That was one of the things that drew him to her in the first place. He and Rylee met when she was a junior in high school and he was in his freshmen year of college at the University of Louisiana at Lafayette or ULL, as they all called it. Somehow, they ended up at the same party and one of her girls tried to talk to his boy. Not only was she dismissed, but he and his boys went on to talk about what they disliked about her. Her friend was nowhere around to hear, but Rylee had her back. She heard every word that was spoken and it didn't sit well with her.

After cursing Mekhi and his friends out like the dogs they were, Rylee grabbed her girls and left. Usually, Mekhi would have slapped the shit out of a female for talking to him the way that she did, but something about her had him intrigued. He told his boys to wait for him while he chased after Rylee and her friends. Mekhi had never apologized to a woman before in his life, but that's exactly what he ended up doing that night. Rylee's friends didn't even know what he was apologizing for. They were just happy to be in his presence. It was easy to make them smile, but Rylee was a different story. She sat in the car and mean mugged him the entire time without uttering one word.

Thankfully, he was able to convince one of her friends to give him some info on her and it was on from there. Mekhi damn near stalked Rylee at school and everywhere else she went until she agreed to talk to him. He didn't care about her lil white, high school boyfriend that she had at the time. He wanted her and he didn't rest until he got her. They had lots of ups and downs throughout their relationship, but that still didn't stop him from making her his wife as soon as he graduated from college. Rylee was only a nineteen-year-old sophomore in college, but she was more mature than women twice her age. She had been through so much in her young life, but she never let anything break her. She basically lost her entire immediate family in a span of three years, but she was still going stronger than ever.

"Are you riding with Buck to go get his cousin?" Rylee asked, shaking Mekhi from his thoughts.

Since Zyra and Rylee had gotten so close over the years, Buck and Mekhi had become good friends as well. Mekhi couldn't really get with Buck's older brothers, Grim and Snake, though. They were always into some drama and were known to be trigger happy. According to Buck, it was his brother who should have been in jail instead of his cousin, Zyrian. It was Grim who shot a man down in front of Zyrian's collision and auto body shop, but the man fingered Zyrian out of fear instead. Being the type of man that he was, Zyrian took the charge, even though he'd never been to jail a day in his life. Sad to say, but the victim didn't even live long enough to see how much time Zyrian got. Snake made sure that he was a distant memory right after he testified in court. He wanted to get to him before that, but he was under police protection until the trial was over with. Once he did what the prosecutors wanted him to do, they had no more use for him. They basically threw him to the wolves and Snake was right in the shadows waiting for him.

"Yeah, he asked me to come with him, but I'm not trying to be out there all day. I might ride back with you."

"Okay, but you know that my cousins are riding with me too," Rylee warned him.

She knew that her husband didn't have the best relationship with her family and she didn't want any foolishness. Rylee often hung out with her Aunt Leslie's two daughters on the weekends, so she invited them to the picnic. Leslie was Rylee's mother's sister, but they were nothing alike. Leslie was messy and known to gossip about everybody in and out of their family. Mekhi hated Rylee's ghetto aunt and her daughters, but he knew better than to say that around his wife. Aside from the few relatives on her father's side, they were the only family that she had left. Mekhi could deal with the white side of his wife's family, but the rest of them could keep it moving.

"Never mind, I'll find a ride back," Mekhi said, trying to mask his frown.

"I figured you'd change your mind."

"What are you wearing? Let me help you find something," Mekhi offered.

He knew that she was about to go off on him, but he really didn't care. Rylee hated when he tried to pick out her clothes or make suggestions about what she should wear. His wife was the most beautiful woman that he'd ever laid eyes on and Mekhi loved to show her off. Rylee had the perfect light caramel complexion, thanks to her mixed heritage. She kept her long, flowing hair highlighted in different shades of brown, and her smile was bright enough to light up a dark room. She had a figure to die for and everything that she wore seemed to be made just for her. Mekhi loved when his wife walked into a room and turned heads. She seemed oblivious to the attention that she received, but he ate it up.

"I don't know yet, but I'm not dressing up to go to a park," Rylee replied.

"You don't have to dress up baby, but you know everybody gon' be out there. Buck said a lot of people gon' show mad love to this nigga, since he was in our bike club before he got locked up. I think he used to be the president before me."

"I'm still trying to see how they made your ass the president. You've only been a member for three years. You can barely even ride a bike," Rylee joked.

"I'm that nigga, that's why," Mekhi replied in his normal arrogant tone.

"You closing MJ's or you got one of the managers running it?" Rylee asked, referring to their sports bars.

"You know I'm not trying to lose out on no money. I got somebody to open and close for tonight," he assured her, as he rummaged through the hundreds of clothes on her side of the closet.

MJ's was a thriving sports bar that Rylee and Mekhi had opened about two years after they got married. It started out being a little hole in the wall spot that people frequented to watch whatever sport was in season at the time. Once when a pay-per-view boxing match came on, Rylee had a brilliant idea. She ordered the game and provided food and drinks to the patrons for a fee. When Mekhi saw how much money they made for the one night, he went crazy. With the help of his wife, they renovated and added on to the place and turned it into a sports bar, calling it MJ's. Since his name was Mekhi Jameson, he just used his initials to name his place of business. The money was coming in and he made sure that Rylee didn't want for anything. She still had her job, but that was her choice to keep it.

"I'm not wearing that Mekhi. I just told you that I'm not dressing up today," Rylee argued when she saw the dress that he pulled out of the closet.

"It's not that dressy baby. I like the way you look in this one though. You can wear some sandals with it, so it won't look too dressy."

"No, I'm not wearing a dress at all. Zyra is going to work me to death and I need to be comfortable."

"Okay, let me find something else," Mekhi suggested.

"No Mekhi, I keep telling you that I'm not a baby doll. I don't need you to dress me. You make me sick with that shit," Rylee complained.

"I know you're not a baby doll, but you know I like to show you off. I need these niggas to see what they want but can't have." Mekhi smiled while wrapping his muscular arms around his wife's waist.

As much as Rylee loved her husband, this was the part of him that she hated. She wasn't the type of person who needed the spot light, but Mekhi lived for attention. He was always bragging about what they had or places they went, and it drove Rylee crazy. She didn't doubt that she was pretty, but she didn't need her husband saying it to any and everybody who would listen. She wasn't his prize and she was tired of reminding him of that.

"I'm married, so I don't give a damn about what another nigga thinks. I'm wearing what I picked out," Rylee said, referring to her denim romper and Tory Birch flats.

"That's sexy too, so I'm cool with it," he replied before stripping down to go take his shower.

Rylee admired her husband's frame as she watched him walk away to their master bathroom. Standing at over six feet tall, Mekhi was every single woman's fantasy and every married woman's dream. He had smooth, milk chocolate skin with dark brown eyes and a low haircut. He was handsome and he knew it. He wasn't modest like Rylee, so he didn't have a problem flaunting it. Having his mother and siblings look up to him only inflated his ego even more.

"This girl is going to drive me crazy," Rylee mumbled as she dashed over to her dresser to answer her ringing phone for who she assumed was Zyra.

When she noticed that it was Mekhi's work phone ringing instead, she made an about face and continued to get dressed. Rylee had no problem answering his private line, but she never went anywhere near his work phone. She knew that, most of the time when that phone rang, it was an issue or some kind of problem that her husband had to solve. Although she was his business partner at the bar, Rylee did most of her work behind the scenes. She took care of ordering supplies and planning the events. Mekhi was more hands on, so he dealt with the managers and the other employees. He was a business and finance major, so he did payroll and other things that Rylee didn't feel comfortable doing. Since she came up with the bright idea of renting out the top level of the bar for private parties, Mekhi's work phone had been ringing off the hook. They were booked up with parties for the next few months. At one thousand dollars per party, they were making a killing. Not to mention how much money the bottom half that was open to the public made every day.

"Please answer that phone. It's your work line, so something must be wrong," Rylee said to Mekhi when he reentered their bedroom.

He had a towel wrapped around his waist and the water had his smooth skin looking like silk. If Rylee didn't have to leave, she would have been all over him in no time.

It was no secret that she loved sex, but time was not on her side at the moment.

"Yeah," Mekhi said when he picked up the phone. He listened intently to whoever was on the phone, but he didn't say anything.

"What's wrong?" Rylee whispered when she saw his jaw clench in anger. That was exactly why she never answered the phone because she knew that it was always a problem.

"Alright, I'll swing over there before I go where I have to go," Mekhi said before he hung up.

"What happened?" Rylee questioned.

"Nothing really, but somebody locked the keys in the office. I have to swing by and open the door with my spare key."

"Okay, well, I'm about to leave out. I can go do it if you want me to," Rylee offered.

"No baby, go get your cousins and do what you have to do. It's not a big deal and they don't need to go into the office this early anyway. I'll get Buck to run me over there before we come to the park."

"Alright baby, I guess I'll see you later," Rylee said while giving him a peck on the lips.

Mekhi watched as his wife walked out of the front door and hopped in her car before picking up his phone. He was pissed about the call that he'd just received and he was about to go off as soon as the other person answered her phone. His anger only intensified when she sent him straight to voicemail. It was cool though. He planned to pay her a visit as soon as his ride came to get him.

Chapter 2

Mekhi sat in the passenger's side of Buck's black on black Charger and sipped from the cup of Cîroc that was in his hand. Buck had gone inside to bring his cousin the clothes that Zyra had purchased for him to wear and, then, they had to bring him to the barber shop. They still had lots of time to kill before they were expected at the party, and Mekhi had another stop to make.

"Where your people at?" Mekhi asked Buck when he got back into the car.

"That nigga coming. He's passing out all of his shit to his boys in there," Buck replied.

"What he trying to do now that he's home? I can probably give him a lil job at my bar, just to keep some change in his pockets. I know that nigga ain't trying to walk around here broke."

"What makes you think he's broke?" Buck asked, looking at him sideways.

"That nigga been locked up for five years. I'm sure whatever money he had before he left is gone," Mekhi assumed.

"Stop always assuming shit. That nigga is far from being broke. He still got his collision center that his daddy was running for him long before he got locked up. He still got his house that he bought a few months before he got locked up too. Zyra and my uncle kept all his business straight for him. And even if they didn't, he still wouldn't be broke. He's straight, trust me," Buck replied.

"If you say so nigga. You ain't got to lie to me,"

Mekhi chuckled.

Buck just looked at him and shook his head. Mekhi was his boy but, sometimes, he pissed him off with the things he said. He was forever looking down on the next man, just to make himself look better. If he wasn't throwing his big house and nice cars in somebody's face, he was always showing his wife off like she was a new toy. Rylee was one of the sweetest women that he'd ever met, but Buck knew that her husband wasn't shit. Mekhi loved his wife to death, but he was a typical nigga. It Rylee found out even half of the shit he did, she would leave him and probably never look back.

"There he go." Buck smiled when he saw Zyrian walking towards the parking lot. He honked his horn and hopped out, waving his cousin over to his car. Mekhi hopped out as well, to get a better look at the man that Buck spoke so highly of. Mekhi sized him up as he walked over to the car. Zyrian was tall, just like he was, but maybe a few inches taller. He had a solid muscular build, probably from working out in prison. Mekhi wasn't the type to judge another man, but Zyrian put him in the mind of the pretty boy type, with his light sandstone skin and low cut wavy hair. He reminded him of the R & B singer Al B. Sure in his younger days, but he had a more rugged look.

It wasn't hard to see that he and Zyra were related because the resemblance was unmistakable. He had the same funny colored eyes as his sister, that Mekhi would have assumed were contacts if he was a female. Buck smirked when he saw Mekhi sizing his cousin up. He hoped like hell that he didn't say nothing stupid when Zyrian got to the car because it would be a disaster if he did. Zyrian was very outspoken and he didn't care about what came out of his mouth. He stayed into with somebody because he didn't believe in sugarcoating anything. He gave it to you raw and uncut, no matter who you were.

"Thanks for the ride cuz." Zyrian smiled, showing off a perfect set of straight white teeth while hugging his cousin.

"You know I got you, man. Here, Zyra sent this for you too," Buck said, handing his cousin the new iPhone that his sister had purchased for him.

"Man, it's been so long since I had a damn phone. I have to learn this shit all over again. I guess I need to get used to that social media shit, just like everybody else," Zyrian laughed as his eyes connected with Mekhi.

He instantly got a bad vibe from him, but he played it off, just in case his first impression was wrong. He swore that he would try his best to watch some of things that came out of his mouth, but he couldn't make any promises. He wanted to ask Mekhi what the fuck he was staring at, but he refrained from doing so.

"Oh, and this is my boy, Mekhi," Buck said, introducing his cousin to his friend, who was standing there just looking at them.

"What's up man?" Zyrian spoke while shaking Mekhi's hand. "Thanks to Zyra, I feel like I already know you and your wife."

Zyrian left out the part about his sister hating Mekhi. He probably already knew, but it wasn't his place to tell him if he didn't. Mekhi smiled and shook his hand, but he also wondered what Zyra had told her brother about him. It was no secret that he wasn't one of her favorite people, so he could only imagine some of the things she said about him.

"Same here man," Mekhi said with a forced smile.

The three men piled into Buck's car and headed out of the parking lot.

"The barber shop, right?" Buck asked his cousin, just to be sure he was going the right way.

"Yeah, I need a trim and a line up," Zyrian answered while running his fingers through the waves on his head.

"Aye Buck, run me to the spot right quick," Mekhi said, speaking to his boy in code.

"You do know that your wife will be at the park looking for you, right?" Buck asked, looking at him like he was crazy.

"Nigga, I know that. Just come back for me before y'all head to the park. It ain't that serious for me to even play with my wife like that. I just need to see what's up," Mekhi replied.

Buck only nodded his head, but he didn't reply. Zyrian sat in the back seat, silently observing what was going on. It didn't take a genius to figure out that Mekhi was asking to be dropped off by another woman. Although Zyrian had never met his wife, he knew she had to be something special for his sister to love her as much as she did. Zyra was a hard shell to crack, but Rylee managed to find a special place in her heart. He'd seen several pictures of Rylee that his sister sent to him, but he had never seen her face to face. Judging by the pictures, she seemed to be the full package, so he didn't understand why Mekhi was stepping out on her. Then, again, Zyrian really didn't know anything about her, other than what his sister had told him. He'd been gone for five years, so he didn't want to assume anything. Rylee was probably doing the same thing to her husband that he was doing to her. Zyrian had seen his fair share of scandalous women and his ex-girlfriend was living proof of that. He hadn't been locked up for a month and she moved on.

"Alright bruh, don't go get caught up in there with that crazy ass girl. You know Rylee don't play that shit," Buck said to Mekhi when they pulled up to the run-down apartments.

"Never that, just call me when you're on your way back," Mekhi said as he hopped out and disappeared into the complex.

Zyrian got in the front seat right before he and his cousin pulled off and headed to the barber shop.

"What's up with dude? I thought he was married to Zyra's friend," Zyrian questioned.

"He is married. That nigga is just stupid. He got the perfect wife at home and out here messing around with these nothing ass hoes. She gon' leave his ass if she ever find out how foul he is," Buck replied.

"So, who is that he's going by now?" Zyrian asked.

"I've never seen the bitch before but, according to the test results, that's his baby mama," Buck responded, shocking the hell out of his cousin.

******

"What the fuck you kept calling my phone for and you knew that my wife was home?" Mekhi yelled to his daughter's mother, Shay.

"You were supposed to bring me some more diapers since last night, but you never called or came over. What was I supposed to do? I'm sick of you always putting my baby to the side for your wife and your bar!" Shay yelled with tears in her eyes.

"She's two years old. I don't even see why she's still in diapers anyway. And didn't you just get paid last week? Why couldn't you buy her some diapers?" Mekhi argued.

"I don't have any more money. I spent my entire paycheck on these bills. You don't help me like you promised you would, so I don't have any other choice."

"So, now I don't help you?" Mekhi asked, pointing to himself. "Who pays for Mekhya to go to daycare? I pay four hundred dollars a month for that shit, but you don't even appreciate it. I don't see your other baby daddies doing shit for their kids, but you don't tell those niggas nothing."

"You can't be serious right now. You got your wife living in a damn mini-mansion, while your daughter lives in the middle of the hood. Mekhya sees you maybe twice a month, but you wonder why she doesn't know you. You hate me, I get that, but why do you take it out on your daughter? It's not her fault that you cheated on your wife and created her. Why does she have to suffer?" Shay asked through her tears.

"You need to be asking yourself that question. You're the one that wanted to keep her. I gave you the money to make her disappear, but you had other plans. You thought that having my baby would change the way I feel, but the joke is on you. You're not the first bitch to get pregnant by me. You're just the only one dumb enough to keep it. Don't fault me for your mistake," Mekhi said as he took a seat on her sofa, looking around.

Although the outside of Shay's apartment didn't look like much, Mekhi had to admit that the inside was clean and nicely decorated. It couldn't compare to what he and Rylee had, but it was nice enough for Shay and her kids. She was doing much better than most single mothers with three kids. She had a decent place to live and a nice car to get her and her kids around.

"Mistake?" Shay asked, snapping Mekhi out of his thoughts. "Is that what you think of your daughter?"

"Look, don't try to make me feel guilty about this shit. I gave you the money to get an abortion and you swore that you were doing it. You let your sister and cousins get in your head, thinking that having my first child would be a guaranteed paycheck, but y'all got me fucked up."

"It would be a paycheck if I put your ass on child support. Or how about I just tell Rylee about her step-daughter that she doesn't know anything about?" Shay threatened.

"Bitch, try me if you want to. I bet all of your kids gon' be without a mama," Mekhi swore. "And keep my wife's name out your muthafucking mouth!"

Shay just looked at her daughter's father in disgust, but she knew not to try him. Mekhi had put his hands on her more times than she could count, and she didn't want that to happen to her again. He put his wife on a pedestal, but he treated her and their daughter like shit. Shay knew that it was all her fault for trapping him with a baby, but their daughter still didn't deserve how he treated her. He did beg Shay to get an abortion when she told him that she was pregnant, and that was exactly what she had planned to do. That was before some of her family members convinced her that having the baby would be more beneficial to her in the long run.

Shay was skeptical at first, being that she already had two kids with two different fathers. Once her sister and cousins convinced her of the amount of money that she could be seeing every month, the decision was simple. She lied and told Mekhi that she was going to have the abortion, even though she didn't have any intentions on doing so. Shay laid low for a few months, until it was too late for her to have to abortion before telling Mekhi what was up. Of course, he was furious, but that was to be expected.

His next thing was to deny her daughter, which he did, up until the blood test came back telling him otherwise. He still refused to sign her birth certificate and give her his last name though. He wasn't even at the hospital when his daughter was born and Shay soon found out why. It was just her luck to give birth to Mekhi's first child on his wedding anniversary. He and Rylee were celebrating in Jamaica, and she didn't talk to him for two weeks after Mekhya's birth. It took him a while longer before he came to see her and Mekhya was almost two months old before Mekhi even laid eyes on her.

From day one, he admitted to Shay that he didn't feel a connection with their daughter and nothing had changed since then. It was nothing new to Shay, since she'd already experienced the exact same thing with the fathers of her other kids. Somehow, she just thought Mekhi would be different. He'd always expressed his desire to have kids, but he wanted them to be with his wife and not her. One drunken night when Rylee was out of town with her family, Shay made his wish a reality. He usually strapped up every time they had sex, but she made sure that he went in her unprotected several times that night. He was so drunk that he didn't even notice the difference. She had so many regrets and having Mekhi for a baby daddy was right at the top of her list. She was getting her payback and it was worse than anything she'd ever imagined.

"Can you just give me a few dollars for some diapers please? I'm tired of having this same argument with you," Shay said in aggravation.

Mekhi reached into his pocket and pulled out forty dollars and handed it over like he was really doing something special. Whenever he had to give Shay anything, he made sure to give her just enough for what their daughter needed and not a penny more. He made it clear that he was not doing anything for her or her other kids. Truth be told, he was barely doing anything for his own child.

"Where she at?" Mekhi asked, referring to his daughter.

"Mekhya!" Shay yelled, calling her baby girl into the living room.

A few minutes later, Shay's oldest daughter came into the room, pulling her younger sister along with her. Once her sister let her hand go, Mekhya grabbed onto Shay's leg and looked over at her father. It was sad that she really didn't know him, but that was his own fault. He would rather keep his daughter a secret to keep his wife happy, so she would probably never be comfortable around him. Shay had three daughters, ages two, three, and four, and none of them had a relationship with their fathers.

"Y'all got her too damn spoiled. Come here and stop acting all shy!" Mekhi yelled with a frown on his face.

"She's not spoiled. She just doesn't know you. Coming around once or twice a month and screaming at her is not helping the situation either," Shay replied.

"Whatever man. My ride is on the way back anyway. I'll tell my mama or one of my sisters to come get her next weekend," Mekhi said as he got up and walked out of the door.

Shay slammed the door behind him, as Mekhya ran back into the bedroom by her sisters. Shay held on to her tears while Mekhi was there, but they started flowing the minute the door closed. True enough, it was her own fault that she was in the position she was in, but she still didn't like it all the same. She was so tired of her baby being some dirty little secret, but there was really nothing that she could do about it. Mekhi's family knew about his daughter but, since he basically took care of them, they played the game right along with him. They all loved Rylee to death and they didn't want to see her and Mekhi separate over his infidelity.

His two sisters and their kids lived with their mother in Mekhi and Rylee's old house. It was the first house that they purchased when they got married, but they'd upgraded since then and let his family occupy the smaller home. He also paid the bills every month, so whatever he said was what his family did. His older brother, Kendrick, was the only one who wasn't down with the games that Mekhi played. He thought it was selfish of Mekhi to do his only daughter that way, and Shay couldn't agree more. Although it wasn't Rylee's fault that Mekhi was doing his daughter wrong, Shay couldn't help but to hate her because of it. If she didn't think that Mekhi would make good on his threats, she would have been told his wife about their daughter. Shay would have loved nothing more than to see Mekhi and Rylee's happy home come tumbling down. He didn't deserve happiness and she couldn't wait until it was snatched away from him.

Chapter 3

Zyra couldn't stop smiling, even if she wanted to. After five long years, her baby brother was finally back home where he belonged. Zyra knew that she was getting on Zyrian's nerves, but she couldn't help it. She kept hugging him and kissing his cheeks like he was a little boy. For five years, she was limited to seeing him for two hours every other weekend, and their contact was very minimal. To have him in her presence with no guards and no time restraints was a dream come true.

"Leave that man alone and sit down somewhere Zyra. He can't even eat without you wiping his mouth and shit," Rylee fussed while pulling her friend away from Zyrian and his cousins. She dragged her over to where she and some of the other women were sitting.

Zyrian and his guests were sitting at the table playing spades, and Zyra was clinging to her brother like she would never see him again. Rylee understood that her girl was happy to see her brother again, but she was getting on everybody's nerves. She was the only female at the table and nobody even acknowledged her.

"I know, I'm just so happy that he's home," Zyra smiled.

"You and me both," Zyra's friend, Brandy, said.

Brandy had a huge crush on Zyrian and it had been that way long before he ever went to jail. He had a girlfriend at the time and he never gave her a second thought. Since Brandy grew up with Zyra, he would always tell her that she was more like a sister to him, even though she was older than he was. Brandy was a pretty girl with a thick build, so she knew that he had to be attracted to her. Damn near every man that she came in contact with wanted her, even if he was unavailable at the time. Zyrian was just different from most men and she had to take a different approach with him. He had a slick mouth, so she had to be careful about how she came at him.

"Your brother is very handsome Zyra," Rylee's cousin, Amber, acknowledged.

Amber was Rylee's cousin on her father's side and the only white girl in attendance. She never felt out of place and they never treated her any differently. Well, Rylee, Zyra, and Nakia never did. Rylee's other cousin, Nicole, on her mother's side, seemed to hate Amber, but she didn't know why. She was always saying inappropriate things to her when Rylee wasn't around, but Amber usually ignored her. Nicole's sister, Nakia, was pretty cool, so Amber mostly talked to her if Rylee or Zyra weren't around. Even Brandy seemed to have a problem with Amber, but they knew not to play with her whenever Rylee was present.

"Handsome." Brandy frowned. "That nigga is hot."

"Yes, he is," Nicole agreed.

Rylee didn't say anything, but she agreed with everything that was being said. Zyrian was that nigga in every sense of the word. If she wasn't already married, he could definitely get it. Rylee was never the type to sleep around. Her husband was only her second sex partner and he was also her last. As good as Zyrian looked, Rylee would only admire him from afar. She took her marriage and vows too seriously to ever cheat on Mekhi. She saw how Zyrian stared at her when Zyra introduced them, but she brushed it off. Even when they hugged, it lingered on a little longer than it should have, but it was all innocent. They'd both heard so much about each other from Zyra, that it felt like they were already acquainted. Of course, Mekhi was right there the entire time, to make sure that every man in attendance knew that she was already taken. They were damn near joined at the hip until Buck pulled him away for a game of spades.

"I hope he's not planning to go back to Dedy's trifling ass," Brandy said, bringing Rylee back to the present and referring to Zyrian's ex-girlfriend.

"You must be crazy!" Zyra yelled. "That was over before he even did his first year. That's exactly why me and my mama went and put her ass out of his house. I would have been a damn fool to let her and another nigga enjoy something that my brother paid for, while he was sitting up in jail."

"And that bitch got like five or six kids now, I heard," Brandy instigated.

"I don't know how many it is, but she got a few," Zyra confirmed.

"Damn, she did it like that? He was only gone for five years," Rylee said.

Zyra had told her all about her brother's ex and how she played him when he went to jail. Thankfully, she didn't have access to his money or the house that he had just purchased one month prior. Not even two months in jail and Zyra was hearing that Dedy had other men coming to the house that belonged to her brother. Zyrian never even had time to furnish it before he got locked up, but Dedy had the nerve to decorate like she would be staying there indefinitely. Zyra and her mother put a stop to that real quick. They refused to let Dedy have that luxury. Zyra was pissed that Zyrian had put the Lexus that he bought in her name because she couldn't take that back.

"She tried it, but I got her mind right real quick. Let her baby daddy buy her ass a house and whatever else she needs. Zyrian better not even try to get back with her trifling ass," Zyra replied.

"Yeah, let him give a real bitch a chance," Brandy replied while popping her thick, glossed lips.

"Brandy, please. Zyrian don't want your ass either. My brother is trying to get his shit together. He ain't worrying about no relationship right now," Zyra said.

"Nobody said nothing about no relationship. After being locked up for five years, I'm sure he need some pussy. And he can definitely get it," Brandy laughed, even though she was dead serious.

"Yeah, him and everybody else," Zyra said, making Rylee laugh out loud.

Brandy cut her eyes over at Rylee and scowled when she wasn't looking. It was no secret that she didn't care for Rylee and she didn't try to hide it. She made it clear from day one that Rylee was Zyra's friend and not hers. She hated how she and Zyra had been friends since elementary, but her bond with Rylee seemed tighter. Zyra clearly favored Rylee over her and it pissed Brandy off. Rylee was the kind of girl that Brandy hated anyway. A mixed breed bitch who thought she was better than everybody else. Rylee tried her best to seem like she was down, but Brandy wasn't buying it. She had everybody feeling sorry for her because of the deaths of her parents and sister, but Brandy didn't have an ounce of sympathy for her. Rylee had a good job and a fine ass husband who loved her to death. They lived in a big house and he'd just purchased her a new car. In Brandy's eyes, she was doing better that most women her age, herself included. Zyra always said that Brandy was jealous of Rylee, but she would never own up to being envious of the next bitch, especially one who was younger than she was.

"Shit, what the hell does he want?" Zyra hissed when she saw her husband walking towards their shelter at the park.

Everyone turned their heads in the direction that she was looking, just to see who she was talking about. She got up to meet him halfway, just so that he wouldn't start anything while her present girlfriend was in attendance.

"You good Zyra? You need me to walk over there with you?" Rylee asked her best friend.

"Yeah, come on," Zyra replied, while Brandy rolled her eyes up to the sky.

Rylee and Zyra walked briskly over to where Tommy was, all the while hoping and praying that he didn't start any drama. Zyra knew that the men in her family would probably try to kill him if he did. Zyra had recently started dating a chick named Mica, and she and Tommy had passed words several times over the course of a few months. He was always popping up and showing out every time they had an event, and she just wasn't for it at the moment.

"What are you doing here Tommy?" Zyra asked with her hands placed firmly on her hips.

"What you mean what I'm doing here? I'm still family, right. I came to see my boy. I had to hear from somebody else that he was home," Tommy replied.

"You can miss me with that family shit," Zyra snapped. "We are not together anymore."

"But, it's true though. Like it or not, I'm still your husband. No matter how many women or men you get with, that will never change."

"Yeah, only because you refuse to sign the divorce papers," Zyra fumed.

"I'm so rude," Tommy said, ignoring what Zyra had just said. "What's up Rylee?"

"Hey Tommy," Rylee spoke without even bothering to smile.

"Look Tommy," Zyra cut in. "Zyrian is busy, but I'll be sure to tell him that you came through. Maybe y'all can hook up next weekend or something, once he gets settled."

"Nah, I don't need you to talk for me. I can go holla at him myself. What, you worried that I might say something to your bitch?" Tommy sneered, making Zyra cringe.

She wanted to slap him so bad, but that would have only caused a scene. Her brother had just gotten out of jail and she didn't want to put him in a position to go back. If she hit Tommy and he hit her back, Zyrian would beat his ass back to his car. Not to mention what her crazy ass cousins would do. When Zyra saw Tommy headed to where her brother was seated, she decided to take matters into her own hands and put a stop to it.

"Zyrian!" she yelled, calling her brother over to where she and Rylee stood.

Tommy stopped in his tracks and looked back at her with rage written all over his face. It killed him how Zyra always tried to make him seem like the bad person, when she was the one who cheated on him. He could admit that he played a major part in the demise of their marriage, but Zyra still took things too far sometimes.

"It ain't even that fucking serious Zyra," he fumed while shaking his head in disgust.

"It's very serious to me. I don't even know why you came here in the first place. What part of leave me the fuck alone don't you understand?" Zyra yelled as her eyes filled with tears of anger.

Rylee rubbed her friends back to soothe the pain that she knew she was feeling at the moment. Tommy always brought out the bad side in Zyra, and Rylee understood why. He was a selfish bastard, and Rylee hated him, just by the things that she'd heard. She always remained cordial, but she had her girl's back, no matter how things played out. Zyra was pissed, but that was nothing new whenever Tommy came around. As much as she used to love her husband, she never thought she'd see the day where the mere sight of him disgusted her. Zyra couldn't help but to think back on when things went downhill in her marriage.

At only 16 years old, Zyra was diagnosed with ovarian cancer. It was very rare for someone in her age group but, unfortunately, that was the case with her. After having her ovaries removed and going through chemo and radiation, she was able to beat the disease that so many others didn't. Zyra considered herself blessed and she didn't take it for granted. She married Tommy, her childhood sweetheart, at twenty years old and things were going great.

Although it wasn't impossible for Zyra to have children, she knew that it wouldn't be easy for her to do. She had already been told that a fertility specialist would be needed whenever she was ready to expand her family. Tommy had been her boyfriend since she was fourteen years old, so he was right there with her every step of the way. He was all for them seeing a specialist, since he was more than ready to start a family. It was expensive, but their only option was to see a reproductive endocrinologist about possibly beginning In-vitro fertilization. Zyra was excited about everything until she was hit with yet another blow. While going through the process to begin treatments, she was told about the huge fibroids that were present inside of her young body. Zyra had them once before, but the doctors assured her that they had removed them all. Sadly, that was untrue and she had to have a procedure to get rid of the few that remained.

That was another disaster within itself. Apparently, something happened during surgery that caused the doctors to make a last-minute decision in order to save Zyra's life. With the risk of her almost bleeding to death, the doctors had no choice but to give her a full hysterectomy, shattering her dreams of ever having children of her own. Of course, Zyra was devastated, but not more than Tommy. For weeks at a time, he'd shut down and go into a full state of depression. Zyra understood how her husband felt, especially since she felt the same way. They always had the option to adopt, but Tommy didn't feel like it was same as having a child of their own. Zyra was fine either way, but she was willing to do whatever her husband was comfortable with.

Their relationship seemed strained for a while and Zyra didn't know what to do. Tommy started complaining about their marriage being boring and, for a while, Zyra thought he wanted out. That all changed one day and Zyra soon found out why. It took him a while, but Tommy finally snapped out of the funk that he seemed to always be in. Zyra couldn't help but notice the huge smile that adorned his face when he came home from work one day. She was about to ask him what he was happy about, but she didn't have a chance to. She noticed that her front door was ajar but, before she had a chance to close it, in walked a tall, light skinned woman with short hair and a huge smile covering her beautiful face. Tommy saw the look on Zyra's face, so he hurriedly explained to her why the other woman was there.

Apparently, she was his co-worker who he'd been confiding in about the issues that they were having in their marriage. Zyra didn't like it, but she wasn't going to say anything about it. That was, until her husband told her the real reason that his bi-sexual co-worker, Mona, had been invited over. According to him, Mona was just what the two of them needed to spice up their now dull marriage. That's if Zyra didn't want to find herself divorced and alone. To say that Zyra was hurt was putting it mildly. She probably would have been more receptive if Tommy would have talked to her first, before just bringing some random woman to her home for them to sleep with. That was the most disrespectful thing that he had ever done and Zyra was done with him.

She packed up her clothes and left him in their house to go stay with her mother for a while. Tommy thought that she was overreacting and begged her to come back home. He even had Mona to call her, trying hard to persuade her to go along with their plans. Mona was cool and Zyra didn't fault her for what her husband had done. They ended up talking on the phone almost every day for a month straight, and she was really a sweetheart. Finally, after almost two months of convincing, Zyra finally decided to go back home and give it a try. Tommy was ecstatic, to say the least. He went all out and tried his best to make his wife feel comfortable. He had rose petals covering the floor, with strawberries and champagne chilling on ice. The massage oils were strategically placed on the bedside table and a box of condoms rested right next to it. Zyra didn't have many rules, but she refused to let the act take place in their bedroom. Their house had five bedrooms, so Tommy had four more to choose from.

Although Zyra was nervous, Mona made her feel so much better about everything. She talked to her the entire time and, after a while, it was like Tommy wasn't even in the room. Once everything was all done, Zyra was eager to find out when they could do it again. Unfortunately, for her, Tommy had no interest in a repeat performance. He'd gotten the threesome that he'd always wanted out of his system and it was a wrap, as far as he was concerned.

But, for Zyra, it was only the beginning. Mona had awakened feelings in her that she never even knew existed. She couldn't stop and Tommy and nobody else was going to make her. For months, she continued to see Mona behind her husband's back and things were going good for a while. That was, until Tommy followed her to the hotel one night and confronted the both of them. Zyra apologized repeatedly and her husband was quick to forgive her. Sadly, that turned out to be one of the many times that she would get caught and have to beg for her husband's forgiveness. She loved Tommy but, thanks to Mona, she discovered her love for women as well. It was his own fault for begging her to do it and Zyra didn't see what the problem was. She never neglected him in any way and they were still very sexually active.

She had the best of both worlds and she wasn't ready to give it up. Even when Tommy gave her an ultimatum, she continued to do what made her happy. He could have easily left on his own, but he stayed, just to make life harder on her. He never laid a finger on Zyra, but the verbal abuse that he dished out was enough to drive her crazy. In Tommy's eye, Zyra couldn't have kids, so she wasn't good for anything else. He kept reminding her that she was the reason that their marriage was falling apart, but she didn't see it that way. It took a while, but Zyra finally got fed up and left her husband for good. She got a one-bedroom apartment and went on with her life. She filed for divorce a short time later when she saw that they couldn't repair their union, but Tommy still refused to sign the papers.

That was over three years ago, and they were still very unhappily married. He eventually had a heart and got himself an apartment, so that Zyra could move back into the home that they'd purchased. His only request was that Zyra didn't disrespect him by bringing any of her women or men to the home that they once shared. That was no problem with her, since she always rented a room whenever she wanted to have company anyway.

"Zyra!" Zyrian yelled, pulling his sister away from her trip down memory lane. "I called your name at least three times. You good?"

"Yeah, I'm okay. I was just calling you over here for him," she said, pointing to Tommy.

"For what?" Zyrian asked, not bothering to hide the scowl on his face.

"I don't know. He said he was coming to holla at you," Zyra replied.

"Man, fuck that nigga!" Zyrian snapped, not caring how his choice of words made Tommy feel. "You and Rylee come on back over here under the shelter."

"Damn Zyrian, it's like that?" Tommy asked with his hands slightly elevated in the air.

"Yeah nigga, it's just like that. Fuck you thought it was?" Zyrian said, walking away with Rylee and Zyra following close behind him.

Tommy stood there for a minute before he finally decided to walk away. He couldn't even lie and say he didn't feel played about how Zyrian had just handled him though. They were tight before Zyrian got locked up, so he knew that Zyra must have given him the run down on their failed marriage. It was cool though. He and Zyrian would definitely cross paths again.

"You got that nigga in life insurance Zyra?" Snake asked, as he and Grim watched Tommy walking back to his car.

"Hell no, so don't even think about doing nothing to him. Let that shit go," Zyra said as she took a seat at the table next to her female companion.

"I'm just saying. That nigga might be worth more to you dead than alive. He don't look like he got shit to live for anyway," Snake replied, making everybody laugh, even though he was dead serious.

"I'm not with him, but I still don't want to see anything happen to him. You can't kill everybody that we have a problem with Snake. That's not how shit works in the real world," Zyra said to her hotheaded cousin.

"Shit, that's the only way it works in my world," he answered, as he once again focused on the cards in his hands.

"I see you took your ride or die over there with you to go talk to him," Zyrian laughed while looking over at Rylee.

"She sure did. My friend know I got her back. We would have jumped his stupid ass," Rylee said while laughing right along with him.

Mekhi watched how Zyrian stared at his wife and he wasn't really feeling it. He didn't even try to play it off, as he stared at her in plain sight of her husband. Being that Zyrian had been locked up for five years, Mekhi knew that he wasn't too familiar with him and his wife. Zyrian didn't know that Mekhi loved Rylee more than his next breath, but he had no problem showing him. He grabbed Rylee around her waist and sat her own his lap, before burying his face deep into her neck to inhale her scent.

"This nigga here," Zyrian said, chuckling to himself. His first day out and he was peeping a lot of shit out already. He'd just met Mekhi a few hours ago, but he could already tell that they would never be friends. Zyrian considered himself a good judge of character and Mekhi was as fake as a three-dollar bill. He tried to make it seem like he was that nigga, but he was really an insecure little boy. According to Buck, Mekhi had more side bitches than he could count, but he clung to Rylee like she was his favorite toy. He felt threatened whenever another man addressed or even looked at her for that matter, but Zyrian didn't give a damn. Rylee didn't seem like the cheating type, but he didn't do married woman anyway. That wouldn't stop him from fucking with Mekhi though. He messed up when he showed his hand, letting Zyrian figure out that Rylee was his weakness. That was one of the biggest mistakes that he could have made. One that Zyrian would make sure that he regretted.

Chapter 4

"Aaah, shit! Baby, slow down before you make me cum," Mekhi moaned as he tightly gripped Rylee's hips and watched as his erection slid in and out of his wife's wetness.

Rylee was in the sitting room watching tv when Mekhi came in butt ass naked and started kissing on her. She knew what was up from there and they'd been going at it all over the house for the last two hours. They finally ended up on the small sofa in their bedroom, and Rylee was putting in work. Mekhi was sitting down, while Rylee bounced on him like she was riding a mechanical bull. She gyrated on him wildly while looking down at him every few minutes to see what he was doing. Most of the time, Mekhi's eyes were shut tight with his teeth biting down hard on his bottom lip. That was about the only thing he knew how to do to keep from screaming out.

Rylee was something like the energizer bunny. She literally never got tired when it came to sex. She was what every man wanted in his woman. A lady in the streets and a true freak in the sheets. Out of all the women that Mekhi had ever been with, his wife was the only one who he couldn't really hang with when it came to sex. He was used to having women climbing the walls, but it was the other way around with Rylee. It was like she was the more dominant one in their sex life and Mekhi couldn't really get with that. He hated to feel inferior to any woman, but that's exactly how he felt with his own wife. It was also the reason why he sought companionship in other women. They made his feel like he was in control and he loved that feeling.

"Sorry baby," Rylee smirked when she saw Mekhi's eyes rolling around in his head.

She slowed down, just enough to make him feel like he was in control of the situation. She never understood how Mekhi was always initiating sex, but then turned around and complained that she was doing too much when she let loose on his ass. She had no problem with her man being in control but, most of the time, he couldn't really hang. Mekhi was working with a monster and he definitely knew how to use it. The problem was that after thirty minutes of putting in hard work, he was ready to tap out and roll over. By then, Rylee was just getting started. Lately he'd been trying to prove a point and go for longer periods of time, but Rylee ended up having to do most of the work. She really didn't mind, but then Mekhi would complain about her being too wild. She felt like she couldn't win for losing. It was no secret that she loved sex and it had been that way since they first met.

"Ughh! Yesss... fuck me!" Rylee screamed out loud as Mekhi began fucking her harder, even though she was on top.

He was putting a serious hurting on her kitty, but she didn't have any complaints. When he pulled her hair and bit into her neck, she really went crazy and started throwing it right back at him.

"Fuck!" Mekhi shouted, as Rylee took the reins once again.

She grabbed him around his neck and pulled him in closer until their lips touched. Mekhi was on cloud nine and Rylee was in her zone. When she started to roll her hips around in a circular motion, Mekhi knew that he wouldn't last much longer.

"Cum for me, baby," Rylee panted as she contracted her walls around him. She damn sure didn't have to tell him twice. Mekhi felt like he was ready to explode, thanks to Rylee and her expert sex skills.

"I'm about to cum baby. You want it?" Mekhi asked, even though Rylee was already removing herself from his lap. She dropped down to her knees and took him to the back of her throat, right as the first drop of semen spilled from his magic stick. It took everything in him not to push Rylee away, as she continued to suck him even after he came in her mouth. He was too sensitive down there and she wasn't making it any better. She literally sucked him dry, and he was happy when she pulled his semi-erect dick from her mouth and stood to her feet.

"Let's hop in the shower and get dressed before we be late," Rylee said, right before she kissed his lips and sauntered off to their master bathroom.

"What?" Mekhi asked through his heavy breathing.

He looked at Rylee like she was crazy because there was no way that he could move at the moment. This was the shit that he hated. It messed with his ego the way his wife behaved after having sex with him. He was sitting there barely breathing, and Rylee was bouncing around the house, acting as if it was nothing. Any other woman would be lying there right with him, just as spent as he was, but not her.

"Did you forget about Zyrian's party tonight at MJ's?" Rylee asked as she walked around their bedroom naked.

Mekhi admired his wife's sexy frame. Rylee was half white but, aside from her skin color and hair, she possessed every feature that a black woman was blessed with. She had ass for days and sharp hips and thick thighs that most women only dreamed of. She had a beautiful face and her attitude matched. Rylee was a very modest woman, but she was a forced to be reckoned with when she got pissed off. She had a mouth out of this world, and Mekhi tried hard not to make her mad.

"No, I didn't forget. Just like I didn't forget that Zyra never paid to have it there," Mekhi responded.

"And she's not paying. That's my best friend. What I look like charging her to do anything?"

"But, that's our business baby. That's a thousand dollars that we're missing out on. It ain't got nothing to do with friendship. That's how we eat and keep a roof over our heads. And I ain't feeling that nigga Zyrian anyway, with that slick ass mouth of his," Mekhi admitted.

Now, he was getting down to the real reason that he was complaining. It didn't have anything to do with Zyra. His problem was with Zyrian. Mekhi and Buck were cool, so that meant that he was around Zyrian more than he cared to be. Zyrian was always saying something to piss Mekhi off. He knew that it was only a matter of time before things got bad between the two of them. He didn't want to put Buck in a bad position by getting into with his cousin but, eventually, that's what it was coming to.

"I really don't care how you and Zyrian feel about each other. This is about me doing a favor for my friend. And a thousand dollars ain't no real money to miss out on, compared to how much they gon' spend on drinks," Rylee remarked.

"I hope your cousins have a ride because we're riding together," Mekhi said, changing the subject.

"Nicole will already be there since she's working tonight. Nakia is coming with her boyfriend, but Amber is riding with us," Rylee said.

"Amber always want go somewhere but don't never have a ride," Mekhi grumbled, even though he knew it would make his wife mad.

"She always have a ride, as long as I got a car. And don't say shit to me about my family because I don't complain to you about yours."

"I'm not trying to argue with you, Rylee. You know you always win anyway. Bring your fine ass in the shower, so we can go for round two," Mekhi said as he got up and made his way to the bathroom.

Rylee laughed out loud as she followed right behind him. They both stopped when they heard the phone ringing, since they didn't know which one it was. Aside from the phone cases, their phone were identical in every way. Rylee's phone case was a picture of her family, while Mekhi had their wedding picture to cover his.

"You need to get another ring tone," Rylee fussed.

"Why can't you get another one?" Mekhi countered while picking up her ringing phone.

When he saw who it was calling, his face immediately twisted into a frown as he shoved the phone in Rylee's hand.

"That's your lil white boyfriend calling," Mekhi snapped.

"That is not my boyfriend; he's my friend. And why does it matter what color he is? I'm half white too, or did you forget?"

"You know I didn't mean it like that," Mekhi said, trying to reach out to grab his wife's hand.

"What the fuck ever!" Rylee snapped. "You can go ahead; I'll take my shower in the other bathroom."

"Why you trying to leave out of the room though? What, you can't talk to him in front of me now?" Mekhi asked.

"I'm not trying to talk to him at all. We need to get ready for this party. I can talk to Brent tomorrow," Rylee answered.

"Whatever Rylee. Just make sure you leave that phone in here when you go take your shower," Mekhi said right before he walked off again.

"Fuck you," Rylee mumbled as she walked away, sending Brent a text message.

She hated when Mekhi referred to Brent as her boyfriend. Brent had been her best friend since they were in elementary school. Their fathers were best friends, so they had no choice but to be around each other. They never dated each other, but Mekhi swore that they were in love at some point. When she and Mekhi first started dating, he assumed that Brent was her man, no matter how many times she told him otherwise. She regretted telling her husband that Brent was her first, but she didn't think it was a big deal. They were actually each other's first, but it was more about exploring sex than anything else.

Brent and Rylee had tried a little bit of everything with each other, and he was the reason that she was so in tune with her sexual needs. She and Brent would sit around for hours watching porn. Once they were done, they would act out every scene of the movie they watched, or at least they tried to. They were very comfortable with each other, but it never went beyond their sexual needs. They were still good friends and that would probably never change.

Mekhi always said that Brent was the one who turned her into a freak. He was intimidated by Brent, but that was nothing new. Mekhi had to always be on top. It bruised his ego when another man had one up on him. He hated to feel like the underdog, so bragging was how he made himself feel better. That, amongst other things, was what Rylee was starting to despise the most. She had never seen that side of Mekhi while they were dating, but it was hard to miss now. Rylee made up her mind to have a talk with her husband the following day. They needed to get some things understood before things got too bad. She would hate for her husband's insecurities to ruin their marriage, so she had to put a stop to it before it was too late.

Chapter 5

Zyrian sat on the upper level at MJ's, enjoying the drinks and music at his twenty-seventh birthday party. He really didn't need a party to celebrate his special day, but Zyra wasn't trying to hear it. She was happy to have him celebrate at home, since he'd spent his last five birthdays behind a wall. The party had just gotten started, but lots of people were already there, with more people on the way. Zyrian looked around the club in admiration, thinking that he could see himself owning something like it one day. He loved how the party area was separated from the rest of the bar, but the enclosed glass area upstairs allowed him to see the happenings downstairs. He knew that Mekhi and Rylee were making a killing. He didn't really care for Mekhi, but he couldn't even hate on him. His bar was the shit inside and out. It was tastefully decorated and the atmosphere was relaxing.

"What's up with your bitch?" Grim asked Zyrian as he went to stand next to him.

"Man, fuck her! That ain't my bitch. I don't know why I let Buck hook me up with her aggravating ass," Zyrian fumed.

"You needed some pussy, that's why," Grim laughed.

"That shit wasn't even all that good. She fine and everything, but I'm not ready for what she wants. She trying to cuff a nigga and I ain't the one. After five years of being locked down, I'm not even trying to be with one broad right now."

"I hear that cuz," Grim replied. "And you know Dedy gon' come running back when she finds out that you're home. She must not know yet or she would have been trying to find you."

"Fuck that bitch too! Ain't no way in hell I'm going back to that. Five years and not one letter or visit. Then, the bitch got a whole football team full of kids now. I ain't playing daddy to nothing that didn't come from my nuts," Zyrian said, making Grim weak with laughter.

"Nigga, you stupid," Grim said as he continued to chuckle.

He and Zyrian continued to make small talk until they spotted Mekhi and Rylee walk through the front door a few minutes later. Zyrian's mouth flew open as his eyes traveled the length of Rylee's body. The low-rise, hip hugger jeans that she wore showed off her flat, toned stomach and belly piercing. Her cropped top displayed the colorful flowers that she had tattooed on both of her sides, giving her an edgy, bad girl look. It was no surprise that Mekhi had his arm wrapped around her waist, making sure everybody knew that she was with him.

"Now, that's wife material right there," Zyrian said, pointing at Rylee.

"Yeah, and that's why she's already married. Don't even try to go there with that man's wife Zyrian," Buck said, walking up on the end of the conversation.

"Nigga, first of all, I don't do married women. They got too many other bitches walking around here for me to settle for somebody else's wife. And, secondly, and let's get this shit straight right now, that nigga Mekhi is your boy, not mine. I told you from day one that I didn't like the nigga and ain't shit changed since then," Zyrian clarified.

At first, Zyrian flirted with Rylee to get under Mekhi's skin, but he was really starting to like her. At first glance, a person would think that Rylee was stuck up, but she was far from that. She was down to earth and very easy to talk to. She had a sense of humor and that's what Zyrian liked about her the most. But, still, she was a married woman and that was a deal breaker for him.

"And you already know that me and Snake never could stand his punk ass. If it wasn't for you and Rylee, he would have been came up missing," Grim interrupted.

"I know how y'all feel about the nigga, but that's still my boy. I know he do some fucked up shit, but he's cool in his own way," Buck said, coming to his friend's defense.

"And like I just said, it's only because of you and Rylee that he's still breathing. Snake been wanted to put him out of his misery. Ole fake ass nigga make me sick," Grim replied.

"And Zyrian, how you checking for somebody else when my girl's cousin came here for you?" Buck said, jumping to another subject.

"What that mean to me? Y'all invited her ass, so y'all need to entertain her. I can't stand a nagging woman. I just met her ass a week ago and she's complaining already."

"Renata is good people though. She just been through a lot with her last boyfriend. Zyra like her, so she must be a keeper," Buck replied.

"Zyra?" Zyrian yelled. "She can't even pick a keeper for herself. You think I trust her ass to pick somebody for me?"

"At least acknowledge the girl, bruh," Buck pleaded.

"I did acknowledge her. Didn't I speak to her when y'all walked in?"

"I'm not talking about just speaking to her. Go chill with her for a minute," Buck pleaded.

"Hell no! I'm trying to smash something new tonight," Zyrian replied.

"I see that nasty bitch Brandy been trying to get in where she fit in," Grim interjected.

"Brandy is a straight up hoe, but she got me curious though. I'm trying to see what that mouth do," Zyrian replied, right as Rylee and Mekhi walked up.

Mekhi looked around at all the unfamiliar faces before his eyes finally landed on Zyrian. And just like every other time, Zyrian's eyes were roaming his wife's body, being disrespectful as usual.

"Happy birthday big head." Rylee smiled while handing Zyrian a gift bag and giving him a friendly one-armed hug.

"Thanks, lil girl," Zyrian replied, calling Rylee by the name that he'd been calling her since they first officially met. Rylee was twenty-five, but she could have easily passed for an eighteen-year-old with her pretty childlike face.

Mekhi had his hand placed at the small of Rylee's back, but he pulled her closer to him when he saw how hard she was being watched. When Rylee spotted Zyra and some of her family at a table on the other side of the room, she excused herself and moved away from her husband. Zyrian watched her the entire time that she walked away and made her way over to where they were. Mekhi really didn't care where she went, just as long as she was away from the lustful stares that she was oblivious to receiving. He headed over to Buck and spoke to everyone, right before taking a seat next to his friend.

Needing to let everyone know that he was in charge, Mekhi called over the device in his ear and summoned a waitress up to the private party area to bring him a drink. Rylee's cousin, Nicole, worked as a waitress at his bar, but she was busy fixing drinks on the bottom level with the other bartenders. She usually kept his and Rylee's glasses filled, but he was cool with whoever came to assist him at the moment.

"You act like a nigga who ain't never had nothing," Zyrian said, looking right at Mekhi as he spoke.

"What?" Mekhi asked, even though he'd heard him loud and clear.

"Nigga, you heard what I said. Everybody know this your shit. You don't have to put on a show for us."

"You sound like you mad or something," Mekhi said with a cocky smirk on his face.

"Nah nigga, dogs get mad. I'm just stating the obvious. They got a waitress up here already, but you hop on your lil earpiece to call another one. We know you own the spot. Ain't no need for all that extra shit," Zyrian said, putting him on blast.

"What you drinking bruh? We got a few bottles floating around up here," Buck said, trying to stop whatever drama that his cousin was determined to start. He knew that his brothers and cousin weren't feeling Mekhi, but they took things too far sometimes.

"I'm good; I just told them to send me something up," Mekhi replied while mean-mugging Zyrian.

Although he would never admit it, Zyrian was right on point with what he had just said. Mekhi wasn't privileged to grow up in a home with two loving parents like his wife did. His father left when he was younger and he hadn't seen him in years. His mother, Carolyn, raised him and his brother and sisters in the projects with the help of welfare and food stamps. His sisters started having babies in their teens and that only made things at home harder for everyone. His brother, Kendrick, stayed in and out of jail and never kept a job long enough to help out.

Mekhi was never a bad child and he quickly became his mother's favorite. He excelled in school and was the only one of the four of them to graduate high school. Thanks to his skills on the basketball court, Mekhi was awarded a full scholarship to college, with room and board included. Of course, his mother couldn't do anything to help him, so he got a part-time job off campus to make sure that all his needs were met. He didn't get a car until he graduated from college and that was only because Rylee's parents had gotten it for him as a gift. He didn't know where he would be without his wife and her family at the time. He would be forever grateful to them, even in death. As much as he'd been through when he was younger, Mekhi felt that he had the right to brag on all that he and his wife had acquired at their young age. He literally started from the bottom and worked his way up. Needless to say that Rylee was the brains behind all his success, but he'd done his part as well. Zyrian and nobody else were going to make him feel bad about his accomplishments.

"Here you go boss," Angel, one of his waitresses, said, handing him a drink.

"Thanks Angel. Do me a favor and see if my wife needs anything," Mekhi said, making her frown slightly.

Angel wanted to protest, but she turned around and walked away without opening her mouth. When she got to the other side of the party area, she heard Rylee's mouth before she actually saw her. She was laughing loud at something that probably wasn't even all that funny.

"Do you need anything Rylee?" Angel asked with an obvious attitude.

"Who is this rude bitch?" Zyra yelled while pointing in Angel's direction.

"Don't you start Zyra," her mother, Glenda, said, looking over at her. She and her husband, Zachery, came to hang out with their son for his birthday, but she didn't need her daughter to ruin their night with her drama.

"I'm not starting nothing, but she got an attitude with my friend and I'm trying to see why," Zyra replied.

"Rylee can handle herself. She don't need you to speak up for her," Zachery told his daughter.

Brandy and Zyra's cousin, China, thought that the whole scene was hilarious. Both of them hated Rylee and they were happy to see that Angel was handling her the way that she was. Brandy and China had gotten closer over the years since Zyra and Rylee had become best friends, and they lived for mess.

"Do you have a problem Angel?" Rylee asked, looking over at the half naked women who stood before her.

"No, I don't have a problem. Your husband asked me to see if you needed anything and that's what I was doing," Angel replied.

"I'm good, but I suggest you check your attitude at the door before you step to me again. If working here is too much for you, you know where the door is," Rylee said, right before she turned her back on her.

"Now, run along and bring us another bottle of this Crown apple," Zyra said with a snap of her fingers.

Angel felt played, but she walked away without replying. She needed her job and Mekhi would fire her on the spot if she pissed off his beloved Rylee. That bitch wasn't nobody special, but you couldn't tell that to her husband. Angel didn't know who Zyra was, but she would be damned if she got a bottle of anything if she had to bring it to her. She had no choice where Rylee was concerned, but Zyra could kiss her ass.

Rylee watched Angel as she walked away with a scowl on her face and wondered what her problem was. This was the second time that Angel seemed to catch an attitude with her, but she was determined to make it her last. She excused herself from the group and made her way over to Mekhi.

"Let me talk to you for a minute!" Rylee yelled to her husband over the loud music.

Mekhi stood up and followed his wife over to a corner to see what had her looking so upset. "What's wrong?" he asked.

"That's what I'm trying to figure out. Angel got one more time to catch an attitude with me and she gon' be looking for another job. I don't know what her problem is, but you better check that bitch before I do. She really got me hot right about now," Rylee snapped.

"I told her to come and see if you were straight."

"Yeah, but she came over there on some other shit. I'm trying to remain professional, but you already know that I ain't the one. I'll drag that bitch out of here by that matted ass wig on her head," Rylee fumed.

"Don't even trip baby, you already know I'm on it. Go enjoy your friends. I'm going to look for her stupid ass right now," Mekhi promised.

Rylee walked away, while Mekhi headed down the spiraled staircase in search of one of his employees. He also took the time to make sure that everything was running smoothly. Nicole and some of the other workers were busy fulfilling drink orders, while a few waitresses took food orders and cleaned up some of the unoccupied tables. The kitchen area wasn't huge, but it was big enough for them to cook and serve the wings, fries, and other small appetizers that they offered. Mekhi looked around for Angel, but he didn't see her anywhere.

Just when he was about to give up and go back upstairs, he saw her coming from the employees break area in the back. They briefly made eye contact, right before he walked up to her. He made sure that Nicole was occupied before he grabbed Angel's arm and pulled her away.

"What are you pulling on me for?" Angel asked as she yanked her arm from his grasp.

"I need to talk to you for a minute," Mekhi demanded as he headed towards his office with her following close behind him.

"What's up?" Angel asked as soon as they were alone.

"You got a muthafucking problem?" Mekhi asked with his face contorted into a mean scowl.

"What do you mean?" Angel asked, feigning ignorance.

"Don't try to play dumb with me, girl. You better not ever come at my wife sideways again. Whatever problem you have, you better get over that shit and quick. You better be lucky that your ass still got a job. She was most definitely talking about firing you. And don't look for me to help you cause ain't nothing I can do if she wants you gone."

"Why would you even send me at your wife knowing how I feel about the situation?" Angel said, shaking her head in disgust. She refused to shed any more tears over Mekhi. She'd done enough of that in the year that they'd been messing around and she was tired.

"I don't give a fuck how you feel. You knew what it was when we started this shit. Half of this bar belongs to her, whether you like it or not. Whatever the fuck she says is the law up in this bitch. If you don't like it, then you need to be looking for yourself another job," Mekhi argued.

"So, it's like that Mekhi?" Angel asked, trying to mask the hurt in her voice.

"It's just like that. Take it or leave it," Mekhi stated in a matter-of-fact tone.

"Cool, maybe I do need to find another job because this one ain't working out like I thought it would."

"That's what's up. Just let one of the managers know when your last day will be, so we can be looking for somebody else to replace you," Mekhi said as he opened the door for her to walk out.

He walked away, but Angel retreated to the bathroom to get herself together. She promised herself that she wouldn't cry, but she couldn't help it. She was the dummy who fell in love with a married man, so it was her own fault. She didn't have a reason to dislike Rylee and she was wrong for how she treated her. After all, it wasn't Rylee's fault that she loved a man who clearly didn't love her. Mekhi had shown her time and time again that Rylee was his top priority, but she still ran after him like a fool. Even when she ended up pregnant by him a few months ago, he made no attempts to be with her. He threw her a few hundred dollars to get rid of it and gave her a job at his bar just to shut her up. That was his way of keeping money in her pockets without actually giving it to her. That also gave him full access to her whenever he wanted her, without them getting caught. Rylee's cousin, Nicole, was the only one who they had to worry about, but Mekhi made sure that she and Angel never really worked the same shift.

After about fifteen minutes, Angel walked out of the bathroom with a smile on her face, as if nothing had ever happened. She was pissed, but she also needed her job. She was living with her sister, but she still had to pay her way. She refused to let Mekhi ruin her night while he continued to enjoy his. She grabbed a bottle of Crown Apple and put it in a bucket of ice, right before she walked back upstairs.

"Here you go. Sorry it took so long," Angel said as she handed the bucket and bottle over to Zyra.

"Thanks," Zyra said, noticing the change in her demeanor.

"Sorry about earlier Rylee. I was just having a bad day," Angel said lowly so that only Rylee could hear her.

"It's cool Angel. We all have bad days, but I hope you feel better." Rylee smiled.

"Thanks, I do," she replied, feeling bad for how she behaved earlier. Rylee was so sweet that she made it hard for anyone to dislike her. She had a bit of a mean streak in her, but a person would never know unless they provoked her. She had a dog for a husband, but she was clueless to that, as were so many others.

"Y'all come on, so I can cut this cake before I go," Glenda said to Rylee and Zyra. She knew that they would be partying all night and she was ready to get home. Her husband would have been in the bed by now, and she was getting sleepy herself.

Zyra and everyone else followed her parents to the other side of the room where Zyrian and the rest of his guests were seated. Glenda could tell that her son was drunk or very close to it. She didn't want to put a damper on his fun, but she wanted him to be careful as well. After losing her oldest son to gun violence, she was kind of overprotective with Zyrian and Zyra.

"Don't y'all let my baby drive himself home," Glenda whispered to Rylee and Zyra.

"We'll make sure he gets home in one piece," Rylee promised.

Zyrian had been staying with Zyra since he got home, so his sister would make sure he got home safe. He still hadn't taken the time to furnish his own house and it didn't seem like he wanted to.

"You want us to take your gifts home Zyrian?" his father asked, referring to the cards and gift bags that lined the table.

"He never even opened them yet," Zyra fussed.

"I'll open them later. Well, all except for this one." He smiled, referring to the bag that Rylee had given him.

The gift said that it was from both Mekhi and Rylee, but Mekhi didn't even know what his wife had picked out. Rylee had great taste, so he wasn't too worried about what was in the bag. Truth be told, he was just as curious as everyone else was to see what it was.

"That's what's up. Thanks Ma." Zyrian smiled as he examined the gift that Rylee had given him.

"You're welcome," Mekhi replied before his wife could say anything.

Zyrian cut his eyes at him with a knowing smirk on his face. He knew that his gift was all Rylee's doing, but he let her husband have his little spotlight moment. Mekhi's jaw clenched in anger, but he tried hard to keep a nonchalant look on his face. There was no way in hell that he would have given Zyrian the gift that Rylee had chosen to give him. A card with a few dollars in it would have been good, but she did way too much for a nigga that they barely knew.

"Please don't open mine. I don't want nobody but you to see that," Brandy said flirtatiously, referring to the explicit items that she had wrapped up in a box. She had purchased everything from condoms to edible massage oils, and she couldn't wait for the day to use it all on Zyrian.

"We'll take the rest of this home with us and you can pick it up tomorrow," Glenda told her son. After cutting a few pieces of cake, her husband and his nephews helped her carry everything to the car.

"You and Snake better not start no shit boy," Zachery told Grim, as he and Buck loaded his truck up with Zyrian's gifts.

Buck, Grim, and Snake were his oldest sister, Donna's, sons and he was surprised that they hadn't given her a heart attack yet. China was her only daughter, but she was just as crazy as the boys. Buck wasn't too bad, but the oldest two were walking, talking disasters. He was always helping his sister bail them out of jail for one thing or another and he was tired of it. He already had to bury his first-born son and namesake, but he didn't want his sister to have to go through that. Not to mention, they almost lost Zyra to cancer and Zyrian to a terrible car accident when he was younger. He wasn't trying to grieve the loss of another family member.

"Nobody not trying to start nothing out here. We're celebrating Zyrian's birthday and then we're going home," Grim promised.

"Ok and y'all take care of my baby," Glenda said for the hundredth time that night.

"He's in good hands Auntie," Buck said before he kissed her cheek and watched as they pulled off.

Buck hoped and prayed that nothing popped off that night. Mekhi tried to play it off, but he could tell that he wasn't feeling the gift that Rylee had given to Zyrian. He saw the look of anger on his face, and Zyrian wasn't making it any better by rubbing it in his face. Then, the fact that his cousin couldn't keep his eyes off Rylee was something else that he was worried about. He saw that Brandy was trying to get his attention and he hoped that her advances worked, since Zyrian obviously wasn't feeling his girl's cousin. Any little distraction would do, just to get his cousin's mind and eyes off his best friend's wife.

Chapter 6

Rylee moved around her huge kitchen, preparing breakfast while doing her last load of laundry. It was the weekend and that's when she did most of her errands and house work. Saturdays and Sundays were also the only days that she had time to cook breakfast for her husband, since she had to be at work so early on the week days. She usually cooked dinner every night, unless Mekhi took her out to eat somewhere. An entire week had passed since Zyrian had his party at MJ's and everyone seemed to have had a good time. Even Mekhi seemed to enjoy himself, but things between him and Rylee seemed off after that. He was his normal attentive self as long as they were around other people, but he seemed angry and distant when they were home alone. Rylee kept asking him if he was okay and he swore to her that he was. After a few days of getting nowhere with her husband, Rylee gave up and decided to let it go. She figured that Mekhi would come to her whenever he was ready to talk.

"Hey Carolyn," Rylee said, answering the phone for her mother-in-law.

"Hey baby," Carolyn replied. "Is my son around?"

"He's still sleeping. You want me to tell him to call you when he gets up?"

"No, I was just calling to tell him that y'all have some mail here," Carolyn replied.

"Okay, I'll swing by there to get it before I go to my grandma's house," Rylee offered, since she already knew what kind of mail it was. She was already dressed to run some errands, so she would add stopping by Carolyn's house to her to-do list.

The only mail that she and Mekhi received at that house were the bills that they still paid faithfully every month. The house was still in both of their names and so were the bills. Carolyn, her two daughters, and their kids lived there, but they didn't pay for anything other than food and household items. She and Mekhi paid all the bills, including the homeowner's insurance. Rylee didn't mind because she would have done the same thing for her parents if they were still alive and needed her help. Rylee's grandmother was on a fixed income, so she helped her out all the time.

"Thanks baby, I'll see you later," Carolyn said, breaking Rylee from her thoughts.

"Okay," Rylee replied right before she hung up.

She had just taken Mekhi's omelet off the stove when he walked into the kitchen. The breakfast potatoes and sausages were warming in the oven, so his timing was perfect.

"Good Morning," Rylee said, right as he opened the refrigerator and pulled out the orange juice.

"Good Morning," he replied in his newfound nonchalant tone.

"Breakfast is ready. Sit down so you can eat something."

"Nah, I'm good on that. I'll eat some cereal," Mekhi said, pissing her off.

"So, I slaved over a hot stove to fix you breakfast and you would rather eat cereal instead?"

"You talking like I asked you to do that shit."

"You didn't have to ask me. Cooking breakfast is what a wife does for her husband. You never asked before, but you never had a problem eating it once it was cooked either."

"Alright, but I don't want a heavy breakfast today. I'm good with just cereal."

"Fuck you, Mekhi!" Rylee yelled as she started dumping the perfectly good breakfast down the garbage disposal.

"What's all that for?" Mekhi questioned.

"I know I bleed every month, but you've been walking around here like you're the one with the period. I'm not about to pacify a grown ass twenty-eight-year-old man. I'm tired of asking what's wrong with you, only for you to turn around and say nothing. Right about now, my attitude is like fuck you and whatever the problem is."

"Who the fuck are you talking to like that?" Mekhi yelled as he towered over his wife as she washed the dirty dishes.

"And you're standing over me for what? Nigga, I wish you even look like you're trying to raise your hand to me. This knife will be in your chest faster than you can blink your eyes," Rylee threatened.

"You better stop talking to me like I'm a fucking child, Rylee."

"Well, stop acting like a fucking child Mekhi. I'm really over your stupid ass attitude. I got shit to do and arguing with you is not on the list," Rylee said as she grabbed her keys and purse before heading for the door.

"Where you going Rylee?" Mekhi asked.

"None of your damn business. Go back to not speaking like you've been doing for the past few days."

"So, I guess you're going by your bisexual, bipolar friend and her brother that you're crushing on," Mekhi said, stopping Rylee in her tracks.

"Oh, so that's what the attitude is for? You think I'm crushing on Zyrian? Are you fucking serious right now Mekhi?" Rylee asked, firing off questions one after the other.

"I'm dead ass serious. You think I don't see how that nigga be watching you all the time?"

"Probably the same way that other bitches watch you. None of us can control how another person looks at us, Mekhi. I've never cheated on you even before we were married and I've never done anything to indicate that I ever would. You sound insecure and stupid as hell right now."

"How do you expect me to feel Rylee? You bought this nigga a fucking thousand-dollar gift!" Mekhi yelled angrily.

"Oh okay, so now we're getting down to the real reason that you're angry. Now, it's all starting to make sense. You've been having this funky ass attitude ever since the night of Zyrian's party and, now, I know why."

"You damn right that's why. How would you feel if I did some shit like that with another female?" Mekhi questioned. "Me and that nigga don't even get along and you do some dumb shit like that."

"But, did I not ask you what you wanted me to get him for his birthday gift? I even asked you how much you wanted me to spend. You were the one who said for me to get a gift that would top what everybody else was getting. If you stop trying to outdo everybody all the time, we wouldn't have had this problem to begin with," Rylee said, arguing her point.

"But, Gucci though Rylee? You got that nigga a pair of high tops with the matching belt. I would have never spent that kind of money on a nigga that I don't even fuck with. I could see if it was Buck, but I don't fuck with that nigga Zyrian like that."

"You should be happy. At least you got what you wanted. The spotlight was on you. Isn't that what you live for? You were the biggest baller in the room that night. That's what you were going for, right?" Rylee asked, pissing him off.

"You call yourself trying to be funny Rylee?"

"No, I'm actually being very serious right now. You always want to be the center of attention, but the shit backfired on your ass this time. It killed you for people to think that you got Zyrian such an expensive gift, knowing that y'all don't get along. That's what you get for always showing off for everybody."

"So, you spend my hard-earned money on another nigga and it's my fault?" Mekhi asked, pointing to himself.

"It sure is. You should have gone with me or told me how much to spend, and we wouldn't even be having this conversation."

"I assumed that you were going to put a few dollars in card or something!" Mekhi yelled.

"I bet you won't make that mistake again, will you?" Rylee said smugly.

"But, tell me something Rylee, since you always poppin' off at the mouth. How do you even know what size that nigga wears? You been talking to him behind my back or what?"

"Wow," Rylee chuckled sarcastically. "I could have sworn I married a grown ass man and not some insecure little boy. Are you sure it's not your guilty conscience that's making you accuse me? It seems like you're trying to shift the blame on me, when clearly I've done nothing wrong.

Zyrian's sister is my best friend, so finding out his size wasn't that hard."

"Whatever Rylee," Mekhi said, waving her off.

"You're right, it is whatever. I have some errands to run. I'll be back later," Rylee said as she turned and walked out of their front door.

*****

Kendra and her brother, Kendrick, sat on the front porch of the house, passing a blunt back and forth between the two of them. Their other sister, Mena, was inside with their mother, Carolyn, and the kids. Carolyn hated when they smoked in the house, so they took it to the front porch whenever Kendrick came over.

"Oh shit, here comes Rylee. Let me call mama and tell her to make sure Mekhya stays in the room," Kendra said as she dialed her mother's number.

"That's really fucked up how y'all be hiding that lil girl like she's a puppy and shit. That nigga Mekhi is foul for real." Kendrick frowned.

"He's not foul; that bitch Shay is foul for trapping him with a baby," Kendra replied.

"You can't be serious. That nigga shouldn't have cheated and none of this would be happening. Y'all know he's wrong but, since he's paying all the bills and shit, everybody is cool with it. Rylee is too good for his selfish ass."

"How can you be jealous of your own little brother? Right or wrong, he's still family. If it wasn't for him, all of us would still be living in that dirty ass three-bedroom project," Kendra fussed.

"No, y'all would be living in the projects, not me. And that's only because y'all lazy asses don't want to work. You, mama, and Mena have never held down a job long enough to even get an income tax. Y'all would rather depend on Mekhi to come around and throw y'all him and Rylee's scraps. Then, the nigga act like he's God or something because he's keeping a roof over y'all heads."

"You talking all that shit, but you be knocking on this same door when that bitch you mess with put your ass out. And shut up talking about this until Rylee leaves," Kendra said, right as Rylee got out of her car and walked over to them.

"Hey y'all," Rylee spoke to her brother and sister-in-law.

"What's up sis?" Kendrick smiled.

"Hey boo," Kendra said right before Rylee walked inside of the house.

Rylee walked into the house and found Carolyn stretched out on the sofa watching television. She looked around the house and noticed that not much had changed since she and Mekhi moved out three years ago. The only difference now was that the furniture that they left behind was now worn and dirty. The carpet was also filthy and the place was never clean, to say that so many adults lived there. Rylee was used to both of her parents working, so seeing how lazy Carolyn and her daughters were was something new to her. Even though Mekhi begged her to stop working, she could never see herself sitting home all day depending on somebody else to take care of her. Mekhi paid all the bills, so Rylee let her bi-weekly paychecks go straight to the savings account that he didn't know about. It was a joint account that she had with her grandmother right after the death of her parents. Her grandmother insisted that she put some money up for a rainy day, so Rylee obeyed her orders. Her grandmother, Sara, was from the old school and believed that a woman shouldn't let her man know everything about her finances. Rylee remembered hearing her tell her mother the exact same thing. Sara didn't care that Leela was married to her son. She needed her own stash of cash and she made sure she had one.

"My crazy ass son just called here looking for you," Carolyn said as she handed Rylee a stack of mail consisting of mostly bills. Mekhi really called to make sure they didn't let Rylee see Mekhya, but Carolyn wouldn't dare tell her that.

"I'm not worrying about your son. I've been ignoring his calls and I suggest you do the same."

"You know that boy loves you to death. He'll go crazy if he doesn't hear from you soon."

"Where's Mena?" Rylee asked, changing the subject and inquiring about her other sister-in-law at the same time.

"She's in the bedroom trying to take a nap. You know her bad ass kids be driving her crazy. Them and their stupid ass daddy," Carolyn replied.

She was hoping that Rylee didn't try to go speak to her daughter because that was the room that Mekhya was in. She would lie down and die before she let Rylee come face to face with her son's secret. Mekhi was dead wrong for cheating on his wife, but Carolyn had her son's back, no matter what. Mekhi was her golden child, or at least that how she referred to him. She was the only one of her four kids to make something of himself. He was financially stable and he took very good care of her. Carolyn didn't have a job and she really didn't want one. Thanks to Mekhi, she had no worries and she wasn't hurting for anything.

Although she hated Shay for trapping her son with a baby, she tried to keep her happy by taking Mekhya off her hands every once in a while. It also allowed Mekhi to see his daughter without actually having to be in Shay's presence. Carolyn knew that her son wanted kids more than anything, but he wanted them to be with his wife. He made a mistake with Shay, but she refused to let that end his marriage. Rylee was heaven sent and Carolyn knew that her son wouldn't have half of what he had if it wasn't for her. She had a mind for business and she knew how to make it work. Plus, she was a beautiful girl that she loved to show off.

"Okay, well, I'm about to get going. I need to spend some time with my grandma."

"Alright baby, tell Ms. Sara that I said hello and I'm waiting for another cake," Carolyn said as she walked Rylee to the door. Sara was an old white woman, but she could bake a pound cake that would put anybody to shame. She would always send Carolyn one around the holidays but, if she asked, she would bake her one any time.

"Okay, bye y'all," Rylee said to her in-laws.

Carolyn was able to breathe easier once Rylee got in her car and sped away. She'd dodged another bullet and she was thankful for that.

*****

"Hey grandma," Rylee said while kissing her grandmother's soft cheek.

She walked around the table and kissed her aunt Susan and Amber as well before she sat down. Susan was Rylee's father's sister and he was also Amber's mother. She and Amber lived right next door to her to Sara, but they were always at her house.

"Hey baby. I didn't know that you were coming over today. I was going to call you later to see about our travel arrangements for next month," Sara said.

"We can drive if you're not up to flying. I'll rent a van, so we can have enough room. It's up to you," Rylee replied.

About four years ago, Rylee and her grandmother started a scholarship fund at the law school in Atlanta where her sister, Baylee, graduated from. They had an online website where they took donations throughout the year. The donations were very generous and they were able to help lots of underprivileged students. Rylee knew that most of the donations came from her father's associates and friends, but she was grateful all the same. Baylee was all about helping the less fortunate and Rylee wanted to continue what her sister had started. It was always hard for Rylee to speak about her sister, but she always gave the scholarship recipients a little background on why the fund was started. Baylee used to be very active in all types of non-profit organizations when she was in high school. In fact, that was how she'd met her boyfriend, Cedric, who became her husband when she was only eighteen years old.

To Rylee and her parents, Baylee and Cedric had the perfect marriage. They would have never known that Cedric was using Baylee for his personal punching bag almost every day for years. They probably would have never known if she hadn't been admitted to the hospital after one of her many beatings. Rylee's parents were furious and they demanded that she leave Cedric and file for a divorce. Baylee didn't object and she was happy to do what her parents wanted her to do. She packed up her belongings and moved back in with her parents the minute she was released from the hospital. She got a restraining order on her husband and tried to go on with her life. Unfortunately, Cedric wasn't having that. He tried everything in his power to get his wife back, but her mind was made up. She was done with their abusive marriage and she wanted out. It didn't really hit him until he was served with divorce papers on what would have been their fifth wedding anniversary.

Cedric went into a deep depression after that. It was then that he decided that he didn't want to life without his wife. He also decided that he would rather see her dead than be happy with another man. The morning of her death, Baylee went to the same university that she'd graduated from to do some volunteer work. Sadly, she never even made it out of her car. A single bullet to the head from her estranged husband's gun ended her life right in the university's parking lot. And if that wasn't bad enough, Cedric got into her car on the passenger side and shot himself in the head as well. Aside for the note that he'd left, the entire ordeal was caught on the campus' security cameras.

Rylee's parents were never the same after that and neither was she. Not long after that, her mother was diagnosed with cancer and things only went downhill from there. After losing his oldest daughter and his wife, Rylee's father, Ryan, basically grieved himself to death. They called it a heart attack, but she called it a broken heart.

"Rylee!" Sara yelled, bringing her granddaughter back to the present.

"I'm sorry grandma. What did you say?" Rylee asked.

"I said that we can drive. I'm starting to hate flying," Sara repeated.

"Mama, you know that's almost eight hours in a car, right?" Susan questioned her mother.

"Yeah, but I can manage. I just hate having to get damn near naked at the airport. We can take turns driving and have girl talk," Sara laughed.

"Who is we? You don't even drive anymore," Amber butted in.

"Well, I'll talk and y'all can drive," Sara chuckled.

"Okay, so I'll reserve a nice sized van for us to be comfortable," Rylee offered.

"Is your husband coming?" Sara asked Rylee.

"Does he ever?" Rylee frowned. "I'm not asking him anyway. All he does is complain when he does come."

"Don't be so hard on him Rylee. We all know that it's a boring trip, but it's necessary," Sara said.

"It's not supposed to be fun, but it's important to me. My sister took her last breath on that campus and I don't have a reason to smile when I go there. I'm not even talking to him right now anyway. He's lucky that I didn't throw his breakfast in his face, instead of the garbage disposal," Rylee fumed.

"Baby, please don't do that. You promised me that you were working on your anger," Sara said while rubbing Rylee's back.

"I am grandma. That's why I washed the knife that I was holding and put it up, instead of cutting him with it like I wanted to," Rylee said, making Amber laugh.

"Shut up Amber," Sara demanded.

"Sorry," Amber giggled.

"Have you been saying that prayer that I told you to say whenever you feel angry?" Sara asked.

Rylee knew that it was coming and she had already prepared herself for a lecture. Sara had a prayer to say for every situation in life. It didn't matter if it was for health, finances, or anything in between. She had a prayer in her book of prayers to help you through it.

"Yes ma'am," Rylee lied, avoiding looking in her grandma's eyes.

"Don't you lie to me, Rylee Ann," Sara said, calling her by her first and middle name.

"No, I haven't been saying it because I haven't been getting upset.

"You just told me that you wanted to throw your husband's breakfast in his face and stab him. That sounds like anger to me," Sara noted.

"But I didn't do it, so that's progress," Rylee smirked.

"Don't play with me, little girl," Sara fussed. "You were doing so good when you were coming to church with me. The minute you stopped, all hell started breaking loose. You need to start coming back. I don't want you to go back to the way you were before Rylee."

Rylee was such a hot-tempered person when she was growing up. It took a lot of praying and counseling to get her back on track, but it didn't happen overnight. She was always fighting and getting suspended from school. She had already been put out of two private schools and none of the other ones would accept her. Things got even worse when she had to go to public school. Rylee got into more fights than usual. The white girls accused her of trying to be black and the black girls tried her because they claimed that she was trying to be something that she wasn't. Rylee couldn't win for losing and, after a while, she just stopped caring. She decided to show them better than she could tell them. It got to a point that nobody could tell her nothing without her swinging on them. Things got so bad that her parents pulled her out of school altogether and had her home schooled. She had to practically beg them on bended knee to let her junior and senior years be with her peers. They agreed to put her back in school, only if she went to counseling and anger management. She agreed to their demands and had been working hard at keeping her anger under control.

"I'm good grandma, but I'll go to church with you tomorrow if it'll make you feel better," Rylee promised.

"Good and bring your husband along with you," Sara replied.

"I don't know about all that," Rylee said right as her phone started ringing.

When she saw "Hubby" flash across her screen, she started not to answer, but her auntie spoke up right when the thought crossed her mind.

"Answer the phone for your husband," Susan demanded.

"Hello," Rylee said, answering the phone for Mekhi.

"Oh, so now you finally decide to answer; I've been calling you all day," Mekhi fussed.

"If you called to argue, then you can hang up right now. I'm at my grandma's house and I'm not in the mood," Rylee countered.

"I'm not calling to argue baby. I've been calling all day to apologize, but you never answered for me. I'm sorry about earlier," Mekhi said sincerely.

"And?" Rylee questioned.

"What do you mean and? And what?" Mekhi asked.

"What else are you sorry for?"

"I'm sorry about how I've been acting this past week and it'll never happen again," Mekhi said. "Now, come home, so we can chill. A nigga been missing you all day."

"Okay, I'm on my way." Rylee smiled. She said her goodbyes to her family and headed home to be with her man.

Chapter 7

Three months had passed since Rylee and Mekhi had their argument, and things were finally back to normal. Rylee and her family had gone to Atlanta and successfully awarded over twenty-five thousand dollars in scholarships in her late sisters' name. Of course, Mekhi stayed home, but he offered to go, even though he really didn't want to. Rylee stopped asking him to join her a long time ago. She didn't feel that she should have to ask, since he knew how much the occasion meant to her. Still. She never put pressure on him to go and she never made him feel bad when he didn't.

"What are you smiling so hard for?" Rylee asked her husband as they drove away from her doctor's office.

She had taken the day from work to get her annual checkup, and Mekhi went with her. He had some questions for her gynecologist that Rylee couldn't really answer. She tried to look up some of his questions online, but that wasn't very much help.

"Why do you think I'm smiling so hard? I'm happy," Mekhi replied.

"I just bet you are, but don't get your hopes up too high. Sometimes these things don't happen right away. It might be a few weeks or maybe even a few months," Rylee warned him.

"But your doctor said that it only takes a few days for birth control to be completely out of your system, as long as you stop taking them. I'm throwing all of that shit away, so I'm not worried about that."

After months of discussion, Mekhi and Rylee were

finally ready to start their family. Actually, Mekhi had been ready for a while, but now Rylee was on board with him. She'd been on birth control pills since they first started dating and this would be her first time getting off of them.

"I know that Mekhi, but I don't want you to think that'll happen in the next few days. It might take some time and I want you to be prepared for that," Rylee explained.

"I'm prepared for whatever. We just have to make sure we get it in at least two to three times a day every day," Mekhi laughed.

"Like we don't do that already," Rylee laughed with him.

"Well, maybe four or five times a day. I can't wait to get me a little one." Mekhi smiled.

Although he already had a daughter, Mekhi didn't really have a bond with her like he should have. He never got to experience rubbing Shay's swollen belly, not that he would have wanted to anyway. He never went to doctor's visits and he wasn't in the room when Mekhya was born. He wasn't even in the country when she was born. He couldn't wait to experience all of that with his wife. Rylee would think that their child was his first, and Mekhi wasn't ashamed to say that he would treat it as such. He never wanted his wife to find out about Mekhya and he would do everything in his power to make sure that she never did. Rylee was his heart and he couldn't see himself being without her.

"You must be crazy if you think I'm spending my days and nights on my back trying to make a baby," Rylee said, bringing him back to reality.

"Girl, your wild ass ain't never been on your back since we've been married. Upside down maybe, but not on your back," Mekhi laughed. Rylee was about to say something slick, but the ringing of her phone stopped her.

"Hey Amber," she said, answering for her cousin.

"Guess what?" Amber asked excitedly.

"What?" Rylee smiled, even though she already knew what she was about to say.

"I got a car!" Amber screamed to the top of her lungs.

"You do? What kind?" Rylee asked.

"It's a Toyota Camry. Grandma and my mama got it for me. It's not as nice as the Benz that Mekhi just got you, but I love it."

"Don't do that Amber. Don't ever compare what you have to what another person has. As long as you like it is all that matters. Just about all of these cars have the same features. The name brand is what you pay for and nothing more. But, I'm happy for you, boo. When are you coming to take me for a ride?" Rylee asked.

"I'll come get you later, if you're not busy. Maybe we can go chill by Zyra or something."

"Ok, that's a bet. Call me when you're on your way," Rylee said before they disconnected the call.

"What's up with Amber?" Mekhi asked.

"She got a car. She's too excited," Rylee chuckled.

"Shit, I'm excited too. Maybe now we can go somewhere by ourselves without having to pick her ass up all the time," Mekhi replied.

"Why can't you just be happy for people without all the extra shit? I don't see nobody in your family with a car, but it's cool for you to be their personal chauffeur though, right?"

He pissed Rylee off when he tried to come for her family, when his broke ass family was even worse off than hers was. He was always taking cheap shots at Amber, but Rylee wasn't having it. He would be really heated if he knew that the money from the car really came from Rylee. She had a nice little savings account and she wanted to do something nice for her favorite cousin. Amber was always catching the bus or riding with other people, so she needed a car of her own. She was making straight A's in her final year of college, all while holding down a part-time job as a receptionist at a local dentist office. Rylee felt like Amber deserved a car and so much more. She didn't want her to know who bought it for her, so she was cool with her thinking that her mother and their grandmother got it.

"I am happy for her. Stop always getting upset for nothing," Mekhi said, trying not to make his wife mad.

"Whatever Mekhi. You have anything planned for later? Amber wants me to take a ride with her."

"No, not unless you wanna roll with me to MJ's. That's about the only thing that I had planned," Mekhi answered.

"I'll pass on MJ's. I'll be with Amber if you need to reach me," Rylee said right as they pulled up in their driveway.

"Cool but, right now, you need to come on inside so we can start working on my junior," Mekhi said, making her laugh.

*****

Later on that night, Rylee and Amber were cruising the streets of New Orleans in her new car.

"This is so nice Amber," Rylee gushed as she looked around her cousin's new car.

Amber had a metallic gold, fully loaded Toyota Camry with peanut butter leather interior. The car was brand new with only fifty miles on the odometer. She'd been smiling since she picked Rylee up and she was so happy for her cousin.

"Thanks Rylee. Where are we going first?" Amber asked.

"Run me by my auntie Leslie right quick," Rylee replied.

Her aunt called her, asking when she was coming to see her, and Rylee already knew what that meant. Leslie didn't care if she saw her one way or the other, unless she wanted to beg. Her mother's sister lived at the bingo hall or the casino and was always begging for money. A few times, she'd gone so far as to spend her bill money on gambling, in hopes of walking away with more. Her kids, Nakia and Nicole, were barely making enough to take care of themselves, so it was always Rylee who had to come to her rescue. Rylee remembered her mother having to do the exact same thing for her sister before she died and she always did it with a smile.

Rylee's cousins still lived at home with their mother and they helped out as much as they could. With Leslie, nothing was ever good enough. She kept a different man in her bed, but she was always depending on her daughters to pay the bills. Just like their mother, Nakia and Nicole never finished high school, so finding a good paying job was hard. Leslie was the type to drain a person dry and her daughters were fed up with her. She was damn near taking Nicole's entire paycheck, which was why Rylee gave her a second job working at MJ's. She only worked three or four nights a week, but the tips were great.

"Come on Amber, I won't be long," Rylee said as they got out of the car.

Her aunt Leslie was sitting on the porch, yelling to one of her neighbors across the street. Instead of one of them coming to the other, they yelled back and forth, letting the entire neighborhood know their business.

"Hey niece!" Leslie yelled when she saw Rylee walking up.

"What's up Leslie? Where is everybody?" Rylee asked her auntie.

"Nicole is working at MJ's tonight, and Nakia's good for nothing ass is inside with her boyfriend," Leslie replied.

Rylee knew what that meant too. More than likely, Leslie asked her daughter for some money and she didn't give it to her. Nakia was nothing like Nicole. She gave her portion for the bills and kept it pushing. Nicole let Leslie use her and always ended up broke because of it.

"Hey Leslie," Amber spoke up after a while.

"What's up snow bunny," Leslie replied, pissing Rylee off.

"Don't call her that. Her name is Amber. Not white girl or snow bunny," Rylee snapped.

"It's cool Rylee. She's only joking," Amber spoke up.

"No, it's not cool Amber. Stop letting people say stupid shit to you. She wouldn't like it if you called her a nigger," Rylee blurted, making Amber cringe at her bluntness.

"Calm down Rylee. Amber know I was just fucking with her," Leslie replied.

"That's all you and your daughter seem to do," Rylee acknowledged, referring to Nicole.

Rylee would get heated when Amber would tell her about some of the remarks that Nicole made when she wasn't around. It pissed her off even more because Amber would always tell her days after it happened. Rylee didn't want to build bridges with her cousins, but she wasn't about to let Nicole mess over Amber, especially if she didn't do anything to deserve it.

"I apologize if I offended you Amber," Leslie said unapologetically.

"What's up Leslie? Why did you want to see me so bad?" Rylee asked. She was ready to go and she was ready for her aunt to get to the point.

"You're my sister's baby. I always want to see you. You're the only niece that I have," Leslie replied, laying it on thick.

"Ok, well, maybe I can come over Sunday and spend some time with you and my cousins," Rylee offered.

"That sounds good. I'll make sure I have something cooked." Leslie smiled.

"Cool, but I gotta bounce. I'm riding with Amber and she's ready to joy ride," Rylee replied.

"Have a good night Leslie," Amber said as she and Rylee started walking away.

"You too baby. Niece, let me talk to you for a minute!" Leslie yelled after Rylee.

"What's up?" Rylee asked, even though she already knew.

There was no way in hell that Leslie was letting her leave without asking for some money first. She left her purse in Amber's car, but she'd already taken out what she planned to give to her auntie.

"You think you can loan me a few dollars until I get my check next month?" Leslie asked in a voice slightly above a whisper.

Rylee reached into the front pocket of her jeans and pulled out the five twenties that she put in there right before they came over.

"I told you before that it's not a loan. If I give you something, I don't expect you to pay me back," Rylee said while handing her the money. Leslie's eyes lit up like a Christmas tree, just like always.

"Thank you, baby. You know auntie loves you, right?"

"Yes, and I love you too. Tell Nakia and Nicole that I'll see them Sunday," Rylee said, right she jumped into Amber's car.

"Zyra's house, right?" Amber asked before she pulled off. Rylee nodded her head and they were off to their next destination.

*****

Brandy scrunched her face up in disgust when Rylee and Amber walked into Zyra's house. For once, she was enjoying having her friend all to herself, but Rylee just had to come and mess things up. Thankfully, China was there so she wouldn't feel too alone.

"Yes, Amber, bitch, I love that color!" Zyra yelled when they walked back inside.

They had just gone outside to see Amber's new car, and Zyra was all smiles. Zyra had taken a liking to Amber and Brandy didn't know why. Amber was a corny looking white girl who hung under Rylee like she was her puppy. She had a cute face with light brown eyes and dark brown and blonde hair, but she wasn't much to look at in Brandy's opinion.

"That's what's up Amber. So, I have somebody else to call when I need a ride now," Zyrian joked.

"Nigga, you just got a car and a bike. You ain't about to use my cousin," Rylee butted in.

"Shut up and mind your business lil girl. I might be drunk and need a ride or something. Amber is my girl, so I know she got me," Zyrian said while giving Amber a fist pound.

"I sure do." Amber smiled, making Brandy's blood boil.

"And make sure he give you some gas money or make his ass call Uber," Rylee laughed, causing everybody else to laugh with her.

Zyra's house was full of people, just like it always was on the weekends. Buck, Grim, Snake, and their sister China were there, along with a few more of their cousins. Zyra's father was one of twelve and her mother was one of ten, making their family huge on both sides. Rylee would have loved to be in such a large family, but that wasn't the way her cards were dealt. Her family was small, which was why she cherished each and every one of them. She never knew when it would be the last time.

"It's too many damn people in here," Brandy mumbled to herself in an aggravated tone.

She was ready for everybody to go home, so that she could have some alone time with Zyrian. She'd been trying to get with him ever since his party at MJ's. She almost had him where she wanted him, but it must not have been meant to be. They got a room the night of his party, but Zyrian was too drunk to do anything. After puking for half the night, he passed out in the bed and stayed there until the next evening. Once he woke up, he took a shower and went home. He kept telling her that they would hook up another time, but that time never came. He had Brandy starting to question herself and if she really looked as good as she thought she did. She made heads turn everywhere she went, so that wasn't the problem. It also didn't help matters much when Zyrian came around with other women. He'd been home for a little over three months and she'd seen him with at least five women since then.

Then, there was Rylee. Brandy saw the way that they played with each other and it made her sick. She knew that it was innocent, but she still didn't like it. Rylee already had a fine ass husband who was crazy in love with her and she should have been satisfied.

"I'll have your lil ass coming to pick me up if I need a ride," Zyrian said, making Brandy snap out of her thoughts and look at him. She had tuned out their childish banter until it sounded like Zyrian had started flirting.

"The lies you tell," Rylee replied.

"Girl, don't even try to front. I'll have your ass getting out of the bed with your nigga to come to wherever I am," Zyrian said confidently.

Buck just shook his head at his cousin's boldness. Zyrian had already expressed his attraction to Rylee, but he was doing too much. Mekhi was his boy and he didn't want any bad blood between him and his cousin. Although Rylee wasn't the cheating type, shit like that happened all the time.

"And on that note, I'm out of here," Rylee said as she got up walked down the long hall to the bathroom.

She shook her head and laughed at her and Zyrian's back and forth wisecracks. At first, Rylee thought he was mean, but he turned out to be just as goofy as she was. He was outspoken and, sometimes, he came off as arrogant but, once you got to know him, he was a lot of fun to be around. Since getting out of prison, he was trying to get back into the swing of things, but he was doing a great job so far. He still hadn't moved back into his house yet, but he said that he was working on it. He was slowly getting around to running his own body shop again, so he really didn't have much time. He did manage to get himself another car and bike, but that was about it.

After doing her business in the bathroom, Rylee washed her hands and played with her hair in the mirror. She sent Mekhi a quick text letting him know where she was, before leaving to rejoin everyone in the front of the house.

"So, you wouldn't come get me if I needed a ride Rylee?" Zyrian said, scaring her half to death.

"Boy!" Rylee gasped while holding her chest to calm her rapidly beating heart. "You almost scared me half to death. I'm glad I just peed or Zyra's floor would be nice and pissy."

"So, answer my question. I thought we were cool, but you wouldn't even look out for your boy if he needed help. That's cold. My feelings are kind of hurt," Zyrian pouted.

"Stop being so overdramatic. I'm a married woman. What the hell I look like leaving my husband at home to come to another man's rescue?"

"Not even the man that you're feeling," Zyrian said, getting all into Rylee's personal space.

"Feeling? I'm married, so how can I be feeling you?"

"You keep using that married line like that's supposed to mean something to me. Honestly, I don't even do married women, but I'd make an exception for you."

"I don't want you to make an exception because nothing is going to happen between us. My marriage might not mean anything to you, but it means a lot to me. What if you were my husband? Would you want me to cheat on you?"

Zyrian leaned in closer to her and whispered in her ear, "No, and I would do everything in my power to make sure that you didn't. That nigga ain't hitting that pussy right and you know it. You're curious; I can see it in your eyes."

Rylee jumped when he nipped at her ear with his teeth. His cologne was intoxicating and she was mesmerized by just the smell of him.

"Don't be scared lil girl. I'll only bite if you ask me to. Let me know whenever you're ready though," Zyrian said as he winked at her and walked away.

Instead of going back to the front of the house with everyone else, Rylee raced up the stairs while dialing her grandmother's number.

"Hey baby," Sara said when she answered her phone.

"Grandma, I need a prayer," Rylee said in a hurry.

"What's wrong Rylee?" Sara asked in a voice laced with concern.

"Nothing is wrong; I just need you to give me a prayer from your book."

"Okay baby, give me a minute to go get it," Sara said as she put the phone down and shuffled away to her bedroom.

Rylee waited patiently until her grandma came back to the phone and started talking again.

"Alright, I'm back. So, tell me what it is that you want to pray for Rylee. Is it your anger or that foul mouth of yours?" her grandma asked.

"No, but does your book have a prayer for lust or adultery?" Rylee asked, feeling slightly ashamed.

"Lord have mercy," was all that Rylee heard before the other end of the phone got eerily quiet. She soon found out why when she looked at her phone. Her grandmother's picture was no longer on her screen, letting Rylee know that she had hung up.

"No, this old lady did not hang up on me," Rylee mumbled as she dialed her grandmother's number again.

"I don't want to hear it Rylee Ann," Sara said when she answered the phone. "I don't want to hear whatever sinful mess that's about to come out of your mouth."

"You didn't even let me finish grandma," Rylee whined.

"And I'm not letting you finish either. You will not sit on this phone and tell me about how you're cheating on your husband. Your mama and daddy are probably rolling around in their graves right now," Sara fussed.

Every time Rylee did something that Sara didn't like, she made it a point to let her know that her parents wouldn't approve of it either. It was only to make Rylee feel guilty, even though it never really worked. Rylee was the kind of person that did what she wanted to do anyway, even when her parents were alive.

"I'm not cheating on Mekhi, grandma."

"Well, you must have been thinking about it. And what lowdown heathen got you thinking about sinning with him anyway?" Sara said, making Rylee laughed.

"I feel so bad grandma. Mekhi is so good to me and I shouldn't even be thinking about another man. Honestly, until I met this one, I never did. I don't know what's wrong with me," Rylee confessed.

"Girl, you almost gave me a heart attack talking about adultery," Sara admitted.

"I guess adultery wasn't the right word, since I really didn't do anything," Rylee replied.

She wanted to say yet, but she left that part out. She felt guilty for even thinking about entertaining another man while she was married, especially Zyrian. Mekhi would go crazy if he even thought that she was attracted to him. He'd already expressed his feelings towards the way Zyrian looked at her. There was no way in hell that she could let her husband find out that she looked at him the same way. It was hard not to. As good as Mekhi looked, Rylee hated to admit that Zyrian looked even better.

"And you won't be doing anything either. Close your eyes and lift your hands. We're about to pray and ask God to help deliver you from this evil that's surrounding you," Sara said.

Rylee did as she was told, while listening to her grandmother recite one of the many prayers that was in her book. Sara was a firm believer in prayer, and Rylee was hoping that it worked for her current situation.

Chapter 8

"**S**hit Zyrian, don't stop!" Brandy screamed as sweat poured down her face, almost blinding her.

She was in heaven, as Zyrian held her legs up in the crook of his arms and pounded into her sensitive flesh. It took a while, but she was finally able to get some alone time with him. Brandy had been at Zyra's house almost every day, trying to get at Zyrian. She couldn't understand why he wasn't paying her any attention, but he had a different girl over there almost every night. Brandy hit the jackpot when she went over there earlier that evening and Zyrian answered the door. She was happy to see that he didn't have any female company, but Buck and his brothers were over there playing cards. Brandy stayed over there all day and night until everybody went home.

When she saw Zyrian grab some towels from the hall closet and head for the bathroom, she used that opportunity to make her move. As soon as the bathroom door opened, Brandy slipped inside right with him. He was about to protest until she dropped to her knees and pulled his sweats and boxers down. Zyrian was working with way more than Brandy expected, but she took as much of him in her mouth as she could fit. He was emotionless the entire time that she sucked him off, but it must have been good. If it wasn't, he wouldn't have taken her to one of Zyra's guest bedrooms to continue what she had started.

"Stop all that damn screaming before my sister hear you, girl," Zyrian commanded.

Brandy looked up at him like he was crazy. Zyrian

was walking around with a concealed weapon between his legs and he wanted her to be quiet. She tried to control herself for a while, but she couldn't help it.

"Shit," Zyrian hissed before he released into the condom and stood to his feet.

"I can't even feel my legs. Can you get me a towel please?" Brandy asked as she panted breathlessly.

Zyrian didn't say anything, but he walked out of the room a few seconds later. Brandy couldn't stop smiling, even if she wanted to. She had been wanting a piece of Zyrian since before he went to jail. She pulled out all her tricks and ended up spending over two hours with him. It was almost four in the morning, so she knew that she was staying until later. Brandy could just see herself helping Zyrian decorate his house, before moving in with him. Zyra's house was big, but Zyrian's was even bigger. He must have gotten it with the idea of him and Dedy having a family to raise in it one day. Zyrian didn't have any kids, but Dedy's shady ass started her family without him.

"Here you go," Zyrian said when he walked back into the room, handing Brandy a warm towel.

She noticed that he'd changed into something else, but she didn't speak on it. Brandy had been so busy daydreaming, she didn't realize that Zyrian had been gone for almost twenty minutes.

"What took you so long?" she questioned while cleaning herself up.

"I had to take a shower."

"And you couldn't tell me that? I need a shower too," Brandy whined.

"Cool, let me walk you to your car, so you can go home and take one."

"Home?" she repeated.

"Yeah, home. I'm tired and I'm ready to go to bed. I need to be at my shop in a few hours," Zyrian lied.

He was going to his shop, but not until later that day. His father loved running things and Zyrian let him do his thing. His money was still flowing and that was all that he really cared about. Most people didn't even know that the shop belonged to him, and he was cool with that. He went to the shop a lot, but that was only to bullshit around with his cousin, Buck, who worked there and the other employees.

"I'm good; I don't need you to walk me out," Brandy snapped with an attitude.

"Cool, but I still need to lock the door, so come on," Zyrian replied while walking away from her.

She had an attitude that couldn't be missed, but Zyrian didn't give a damn. He wasn't trying to be up under her ass a minute longer and she damn sure wasn't staying until daylight. She got exactly what she'd been begging for and that was a wrap. Brandy snatched up her purse from the floor and stomped towards the front door like a spoiled child.

"What do you have planned for later today?" Brandy asked Zyrian.

"Sleep and work," he remarked dryly.

She nodded and walked out of the front door before it was abruptly slammed behind her. Although she'd told Zyrian that she didn't want him to walk her out, her feelings were kind of hurt when he didn't. He was a man, so he should have insisted. It was cool though. Brandy got into her car and sped off towards her house.

"Out of all the bitches in New Orleans, you just had to give her thirsty ass the dick," Zyra fussed as she stood at the bottom of the stairs.

When she heard her front door sensor come on, she ran downstairs to see who was coming in or out of her house that time of the morning. When she saw Zyrian letting Brandy, out she wanted to scream. Brandy was her girl, but she didn't want her for a sister-in-law. Brandy was decent looking with a nice shape, but she was a hoe looking for a come up. She didn't care if a man had a wife or a girlfriend; she would bust it wide open with no questions asked. She'd been after Zyrian for years, but he never gave her the time of day until now.

"That bitch pounced on me when I was about to take my shower. But, I hope she enjoyed herself because she'll never get it again," Zyrian promised.

"Why? What happened?" Zyra asked.

"She damn near took all the skin off my dick with them sharp ass teeth," he complained.

"I know she didn't. Not how she be bragging about how she got niggas hooked and shit," Zyra said.

"Hooked with what? I know she ain't out here bragging on that loose shit. I felt like I was fucking a bowl of jello. I've been home all these months and ain't had nothing good yet. Shit, I did better pleasing myself in jail," Zyrian complained.

"You mean to tell me that none of them hoes you been bringing here has made you tap out yet?" Zyra teased. "What about the cute red one with the short hair?"

"Don't even mention that hairy bitch to me. I couldn't even find the pussy through all them weeds and grass she had between her legs." Zyrian frowned.

"What about that girl Natalie or Nancy? Whatever her name was."

"I didn't even fuck her. She smelled like piss," Zyrian said, making his sister weak with laughter.

"And?" Zyra asked through her laughter. "Maybe she's a squirter."

"Man, quit playing with me, Zyra. This shit is just ridiculous," Zyrian frowned.

"Just keep looking. The way you running through women, you'll find something that you like eventually. You have to stop being so picky. You find something wrong with every woman you get with."

"I want your girl, straight up," Zyrian admitted. "I bet I won't find nothing wrong with her fine ass."

"Just let that go Zyrian. Rylee ain't even on that cheating shit. She not gon' mess around on Mekhi for nothing or nobody," Zyra said, waving him off.

"She just never ran across the right one yet."

"But, aren't you the same one that said he don't do married women? They got too many available bitches out here for me to settle for another man's wife," Zyra said, repeating her little brother's words right back to him.

"I wasn't talking about her though. I told you that she's the only exception that I would make. And stop always bringing up old shit."

"Nigga, that was only two days ago," Zyra clarified.

"It don't even matter. I still want her pretty ass. That nigga Mekhi ain't right."

"I don't like his ass either, but he's good to my friend. He's just a show off who brags too damn much. As long as he doesn't put his hands on her or cheat, then I'm good," Zyra replied.

Zyrian only nodded his head because he knew the truth. It wasn't his place to tell his sister or anyone else though. As bad as he wanted Rylee, he wasn't about to hate on her husband just to get her. He couldn't see himself badmouthing another man to his wife. That just wasn't his style. He talked about it with his cousins from time to time, but that was as far as it went.

"I'm going to bed and try to forget that sex with your girl ever happened," Zyrian said, making his sister laugh. They both headed up the stairs and disappeared into their own bedrooms.

*****

"Nigga, you crazy out of your mind!" Buck yelled to his cousin.

He had just picked Zyrian up from Zyra's house, and they were headed to the daiquiri shop to shoot some pool.

"Man, I'm spending money for nothing on a house that I ain't even living it. Then, Zyra act like she be ready to cry every time I mention something about me moving out," Zyrian replied as he puffed on the loud that they were passing back and forth. He was happy as hell that he wasn't on any papers and he could do exactly what he wanted to do.

"Forget Zyra, bruh. She got her own house and you need your own shit too," Buck argued.

"I might get me something else in a few months. It ain't like I can't afford it."

"Nigga, you can afford a few houses. Walking around here acting like you a regular nigga, when you got millions sitting up in the bank. You kill me with that shit," Buck laughed.

"I am a regular nigga. Money don't make me no different from nobody else. And I don't really want to stay in a house that I lived in with Dedy anyway. I need some new memories in a new house. Hopefully, it won't stay on the market too long."

"You just put it up today, so I give it about two or three months before it's sold. That's a nice area."

"I never even enjoyed the damn house before I got locked up. It's cool though. I'm buying my next one in Audubon Place."

"Damn cuz, you trying to be surrounded by the rich and famous huh," Buck laughed.

"I'm just trying to enjoy myself and live for a change. Bruh, I'm twenty-seven years old and, aside from going to jail out of town, I've never been out of New Orleans."

"You got to stop feeling guilty about spending money that's rightfully yours. You got more than enough money to travel the world twice," Buck noted.

Zyrian only nodded his head, but he didn't respond. His finances were always a touchy subject for him and he hated to discuss it. He was happy when his cousin's phone rang because he didn't want to continue their conversation. Buck's phone was mounted to the dashboard on his car, so he pressed the speakerphone button and talked while he drove.

"What's up Mekhi?" Buck asked his boy.

"Man, I need a ride like right now," Mekhi said with urgency.

"A ride from where? And where the hell is your car?" Buck asked.

"Man, I'm at the room in Kenner, but I didn't drive. I'm with this stupid ass girl and her piece of shit car broke down. My car is parked at MJ's and I need to get back like right now," Mekhi stressed.

"Bruh, you might have to wait a few minutes. I'm all the way on the Westbank and I'm not alone. Let me drop my passenger off and I'll be there."

"Man, did you not just hear what I said? I really need you right now Buck. Just bring whoever that is with you. I can't have my wife going to MJ's looking for me and I'm not there," Mekhi panicked. He knew that Buck was probably riding with his girl or one of his other jump offs, but he really didn't care at the moment. He was desperate.

"I'm on my way man. You always doing stupid shit and then be crying about Rylee finding out. I really don't understand you," Buck lectured before he hung up.

He already knew where Mekhi was, since that was the only place he went to when he was doing dirt. This wasn't Buck's first time picking him up and it probably wouldn't be the last. He hated that Zyrian was with him, but he couldn't do anything to change that. Buck knew that his cousin was really feeling Rylee and Mekhi was making the shit too easy for him.

"What his punk ass into now?" Zyrian asked.

"Ain't no telling," Buck replied with a shrug.

"You can bring me back home if you have to; it's cool," Zyrian offered.

"Nah, that nigga sound like he's about to cry as it is. I don't want to take twenty minutes to bring you home and another twenty to get to him."

About thirty minutes later, Buck and Zyrian pulled up to the Doubletree Hotel in Kenner near the airport. Buck sent Mekhi a text, letting him know that he was out front. The two cousins waited patiently for another five minutes until they spotted Mekhi and another woman walking towards the front.

"I know damn well that nigga ain't fucking her!" Zyrian angrily yelled when he got a closer look at Mekhi's female companion.

"Chill out cuz," Buck advised.

"And you knew about this shit?" Zyrian asked.

"That don't have nothing to do with me. I know the situation is fucked up, but I'm not getting involved in that. I'm tired of telling this nigga about trying to put me in the middle of his bullshit too."

"Man, fuck that! You put yourself in the middle by running to his rescue when he's doing wrong. That nigga is foul for that shit. I can't believe this dude is that dirty," Zyrian ranted.

"I get what you're saying bruh, but that's still none of my business. I don't agree with the shit, but he's a grown man." Buck shrugged like his hands were tied.

Even though his cousin was right, Zyrian couldn't help but feel some kind of way. Even if nothing ever popped off between him and Rylee, Mekhi still didn't deserve her. He had one of the baddest females that Zyrian had ever seen on his arm, but he still wasn't satisfied. Mekhi walked up to the back-passenger's side and pulled the door open. He almost pissed his pants when he saw Zyrian already sitting up front. Buck had heavily tinted windows, so he couldn't see who was in the car with him when he pulled up. Mekhi knew that he had somebody with him, but he never imagined that that someone would be Zyrian. He just assumed that his friend had more sense than that. Of all the people to bring, he chose to bring a nigga that Mekhi despised the most. The brother of his wife's best friend. That was a dumb move on Buck's part. Not to mention, Zyrian was ice grilling him when they did make eye contact. Mekhi prayed that he didn't tell Zyra because Rylee would know for sure if he did.

"What the fuck is wrong with her dumb ass?" Buck asked Mekhi when he hopped in the back seat of his car.

"Her stupid ass is mad because I told her I was leaving. Fuck I look like waiting for her mechanic to show up and fix that raggedy ass car," Mekhi replied as they pulled out into traffic.

"Fuck you look like being at a hotel with another bitch in the first place," Zyrian butted in.

Mekhi chewed on the inside of his jaw to keep from saying what he really wanted to say. He really wanted to go off on Zyrian, but he didn't want to make matters worse. He had to stay on Zyrian's good side to assure that he didn't go running his mouth to his sister. Mekhi knew that the siblings were close, but he didn't know how far that closeness went.

"Take me back to MJ's," Mekhi instructed Buck while he sent his wife a text.

"Yeah, and me and you need to link up later on. I need to holla at you about a few things," Buck replied.

This was going to be his last time telling Mekhi about the stupid stunts that he pulled. Rylee was his girl and he didn't want her to think that he was helping her husband do her wrong. Buck couldn't figure out why Mekhi cheated in the first place. He was on the outside looking in, but Rylee seemed to really have her shit together. It wasn't just about her looks. She was a smart woman who was about her business. And according to Mekhi, she was also every man's fantasy in the bedroom. Buck didn't really believe in perfection, but Rylee seemed like the perfect wife who married a no-good ungrateful man.

"You coming in for a minute?" Mekhi asked Buck when they pulled up to MJ's.

"Nah, me and Zyrian already had plans. I'll get up with you later."

Buck pulled off, shaking his head in disgust as soon as Mekhi got out of his car.

"Stupid ass," Buck mumbled loud enough for his cousin to hear.

"Don't tell that clown ass nigga nothing. I ain't even gon' have to go after his wife. He's pushing her right to me and don't even know it," Zyrian smirked.

Chapter 9

"**G**irl, you are too stupid. I would have been told that nigga's wife about my baby if I were you," Shay's cousin, Karen, told her. "I said the same thing. He got that hoe living lovely in some estates, while you and my niece are living in the middle of the ghetto," Shay's sister, Deidra, chimed in.

Shay was already aggravated and her family wasn't making it any better. She hadn't heard from Mekhi in over a month and the two hundred dollars that he sent her had been spent since day one. Even Carolyn and his sisters were acting shady. Shay asked them if her daughter could come over two weeks ago, and they had yet to answer her. Mekhi had forgotten to pay Mekhya's nursery bill and she couldn't go back until he did. Shay had been depending on her sister and other family members to watch her baby girl while she went to work. Thankfully, the other two were in pre-k, third, and fourth, so she didn't have to worry about them.

"And you gon' have to find somebody else to watch Mekhya tomorrow because I already made plans," Karen said, interrupting Shay's thoughts.

"Yep, and I have to work in the morning, so I can't help you either," Deidra countered.

"I'm so sick of this shit," Shay cursed as angry tears spilled from her eyes.

"I fault you for all of this. You let Mekhi throw you a few coins just to shut you up, when you know you could be getting way more than that. He lied and told you that he was living in a townhouse, until we followed his ass home one day and saw how he was really living. Then, he's on Facebook and Instagram bragging about how much he spent on the Benz that he just got his wife. You can't even get that nigga to keep up with his daughter's nursery bill," Deidra said, adding salt to the already fresh wound.

"You need to pop up at that nigga house and drop Mekhya right off to his ass." Karen suggested.

"Bitch, you must be crazy. Mekhya barely knows who he is. He'll never mistreat my daughter, just because he's mad with me," Shay argued.

"Okay, but you need to at least let his wife know about the double life that he's living. That nigga is getting away with the shit because you're letting him. You probably can't even go to work in the morning because you don't have a babysitter," Karen lectured.

"Oh, I'm going to work. You can best believe that shit. I'm barely making ends meet now, so missing a day is out of the question. I bet I pack Mekhya's shit and be knocking at Carolyn's door bright and early in the morning," Shay swore.

"I hear you, but I still think you're knocking at the wrong door. Carolyn is just the grandmother and she don't owe you nothing. I do think she's wrong for ignoring you like she's been doing, but she's not obligated to watch your baby. You want to lay the blame on everybody except for the one who's really responsible," Deidra said.

"Y'all just don't get it. Carolyn and her daughters do whatever Mekhi tells them to do. He tells them when to get Mekhya, how long to keep her, and when to bring her back. He's been all into that bike club shit and he probably hasn't told them much of anything lately. They're too dumb to think for themselves, so they don't move without his say so," Shay reasoned.

"I can't believe that you're still making excuses for him. Honestly, I don't blame Mekhi for doing what he does to you because you let him. There is no way in hell that you should be living like this when your baby daddy is making thousands of dollars a night. But if you like it, I love it. Let's go Karen," Deidra said to her cousin as they prepared to leave.

Shay understood everything that they were saying, but it wasn't that easy. She hated how things were between her and Mekhi, but she wasn't sure about how to approach the situation. She never had to worry about that with the fathers of her other kids because she didn't even know where they were. They stuck around long enough to see the double lines on the pregnancy test and they were done. They were both in relationships when she got pregnant as well, but they didn't have shit to offer her or her daughters. Mekhi was the best one by far, but she still couldn't get him to do right.

Shay didn't tell her sister and cousin, but Rylee was the only reason why she never went to Mekhi's home. Shay's intentions were never to hurt her because Rylee and Mekhya were the only innocent ones in the scenario. True, at times, she got pissed and blamed Rylee for Mekhi's actions, but that was only her anger talking. She knew that his wife had no clue what was going on and he intended to keep it that way. Mekhi was determined to make sure that their daughter stayed hidden at all cost.

"Mekhya!" Shay yelled out for her baby girl.

When Mekhya appeared in the doorway, Shay motioned for her to come closer to her.

"Give me my phone," she instructed her two-year-old, who was playing a game on the device. As soon as Mekhya handed her the phone, Shay dialed Carolyn's number for the fourth time that day.

"Yes Shay," Mekhi's sister, Mena, answered, sounding disgusted.

"Where is Carolyn?" Shay asked, sounding just as disgusted as she was.

"She's still not here Shay. Just like she wasn't here the last few times that you called," Mena snapped before hanging up the phone in her face.

"Stupid bitch," Shay cursed as she jumped up from the sofa.

She went to her daughter's bedroom and grabbed Mekhya's overnight bag. She mumbled obscenities under her breath the entire time that she grabbed clothes and shoes from various places in the room and threw them in the bag. Shay knew that Mena was lying because Carolyn rarely went anywhere. Her daughters were always with her when she did, so she couldn't have gone far. None of them even had a car, so they had to wait for Kendrick to bring them everywhere. Carolyn could run from a phone call, but Shay was done calling her. She and Mekhya were about to pay her a much-needed visit, but Shay would be leaving alone. Mekhi usually determined when his daughter visited his family, but Shay was about to make the decision for him.

*****

"Baby, I need a favor if you can do it," Mekhi said to Rylee as he stepped into the walk-in shower with her.

They'd been ripping and running all day and they were finally settled in at home. After taking his wife on an intense shopping spree, Mekhi took her out to eat at one of her favorite restaurants. Landry's Seafood sold some of the best food in New Orleans, and Rylee loved just about everything on the menu. Afterwards, they went home, where she damn near fucked him into a coma. Mekhi was out like a light after that and the ringing of his phone was what ended his slumber. He woke up to find his wife in the shower and decided to join her.

"Okay, what's up?" she asked as she turned around and began to lather her husband's body with soap.

"We got our bike club meeting tomorrow and I'm supposed to bring some food. I forgot all about it, but Buck just called and reminded me. You think you can grab something for me and drop it off to the house?" Mekhi asked, referring to the renovated house that now served as their club's meeting place.

"Yeah, I can do that. What did you have in mind?" Rylee asked.

"They usually have like party foods and stuff, but whatever you bring is fine. I know it's last minute."

"Amber and my auntie make party sandwiches all the time. I can get them to do that and I'll buy some other stuff," Rylee suggested.

"That's perfect baby. I really appreciate it," Mekhi said while giving his wife a kiss.

Rylee smiled at him as she continued to wash him off. When they got out of the shower, Rylee immediately called her cousin to see if she and her mother would be able to help her out the following day. Once Amber gave her the okay, Rylee made a grocery list of everything that she would need. After grabbing her iPad to finish reading her book, she joined her husband in their bed. Rylee read for about an hour before drifting off into a peaceful night's sleep.

*****

"Dang auntie, you and Amber need to go into business. Y'all got these sandwiches looking like they came from a deli," Rylee complimented.

"I told her that, but she's too lazy," Amber said about her mother.

"I'm not lazy. I work a full-time job and help out with your grandma when she needs it. I don't have time for anything extra," Susan replied. She couldn't depend on her other siblings to be there for her mother, so she never even asked. Aside from her and Amber, Rylee was the only one who made sure that Sara was straight.

"Well, I appreciate y'all for doing this on such short notice," Rylee replied.

"You know it's not a problem," her aunt replied with a genuine smile.

"What are you doing today Amber? Come chill with me for a while," Rylee said to her cousin.

"Her ass ain't doing nothing. If you don't get her out of the house, she'll be sitting in here with me all day," Susan complained.

"Don't listen to her, Rylee. She always wants to get rid of me since she got a new man. She waited until she got divorced from my daddy to get a black boyfriend. I told her she should have done that in the beginning and then maybe I would have some junk in my trunk like you," Amber laughed.

"You got you some chocolate auntie?" Rylee teased.

"No honey, I got me some dark chocolate," Susan smirked.

"I ain't even mad at you, girl. I already know what's up, so you don't even have to explain. Let's go Amber," Rylee said to her goofy little cousin.

She and Amber put the sandwiches in the car with the rest of the food and headed to the Freedom Riders Bikers Club to drop everything off to Mekhi. Rylee had been to the Biker's Club several times, but she felt uneasy about going there now. Since being released from jail, Zyrian was back in the club and she didn't want to run into him. She'd been trying her best to stay away from him and she hadn't been to Zyra's house in about two weeks. She had Zyra thinking that she was busy with her grandmother, but truth was she was scared to be around her brother.

"I'm staying in the car," Amber said when she and Rylee pulled up to their destination.

"Don't do me like that Amber. Get out with me, please," Rylee begged.

"Why can't you just call Mekhi and tell him to send someone out to get it?" Amber questioned.

"That's a good idea," Rylee agreed as she fumbled around in her purse for her phone.

Rylee was scrolling through her phone contacts trying to locate her husband's number when her car door was pulled open, scaring her momentarily.

"What's up wifey?" Zyrian smiled down at her.

"Boy move," Rylee laughed nervously as she got out of the car. "How can I be your wifey when I'm already somebody else's wife?"

"Fuck your husband." Zyrian shrugged like it was nothing.

"Ok, now that you've gotten that off of your chest, what is it that you want Zyrian?" Rylee questioned.

"You," he replied while licking his full sexy lips and staring her in the eyes.

Amber looked just as uncomfortable as Rylee about Zyrian's flirting, but she played on her phone like she was unaffected. Zyra told her that her little brother had a crush on Rylee, but Amber had never heard him speak on it so openly.

"I... um, I have some food for the meeting. I need somebody to bring it in for me," Rylee stammered unintentionally.

"Do I make you nervous Rylee?" Zyrian asked with a cocky smirk on his face.

He walked up to her and closed the small gap that separated the two of them. Rylee tried to stop herself from staring at his lips but, every time his tongue ran across them, her eyes seemed to follow. She wasn't shy at all, but Zyrian made her nervous for some reason. Maybe it was because she was a married woman who was secretly lusting over another man. A man that she tried hard to avoid at all cost. A man who damn near had her standing in a puddle of her own juices. Trying to stay away from him was one of the best decisions that she ever made.

"I didn't know that you were out here baby," Mekhi said as he walked over and broke up the intense stare down that Zyrian was having with his wife. He was pissed but decided not to make a scene in front of everyone. He was sure that the other club members witnessed the encounter and that was just as embarrassing as seeing it himself.

"Yeah, I was just about to call you," Rylee replied in a shaky voice.

Zyrian chuckled when he saw Mekhi grab Rylee's small waist and pin her up against the car. He lowered his lips to hers and engaged in a deep kiss that almost took her breath away. Rylee knew that he was only behaving like that because Zyrian was right there, but she had to go with the flow. Rylee knew that she and Mekhi would probably be arguing later that night, but she didn't care.

"What did you need me to help you with Rylee?" Zyrian interrupted once he had enough of their face sucking. Rylee pulled away from her husband and wiped her lips before she replied. Mekhi looked like he wanted to say something, but he kept his mouth closed.

"I have some food for y'all greedy asses in the back of my car," she joked.

Amber got out of the car and started grabbing food, along with Mekhi, Zyrian, and Rylee. They all walked into the house and put everything on the table before Rylee and Amber turned to walk back outside. Amber was scared out of her mind when one of the men grabbed her arm as she walked down the stairs.

"Who is your friend Rylee?" one of the bikers, who was also Zyra and Zyrian's cousin, asked.

"That's my cousin and I need you to let her arm go. If you want to know her name, just ask her," Rylee replied.

"Your cousin?" one of the other men questioned with a loud laugh.

"Yes, my first cousin actually. Is there something funny about that?" Rylee asked as she turned to face him. He must have been new because she had never seen him before. Just about everybody there knew that she had both black and white family members and none of them ever said anything stupid. When the unknown man kept laughing, Rylee was ready to go off on him, but she never got the chance.

"Nigga, you better go sit your fat ass down somewhere! You always fucking with somebody!" Zyrian yelled to the man as he and Mekhi came back outside. He never even gave Mekhi a chance to defend his own wife before he stepped up.

"I got this. I don't need you to speak up for my wife," Mekhi said as he mugged Zyrian.

"Shit, nigga, you don't act like it," Zyrian replied while walking back to the house.

Mekhi shook his head in anger as he walked Rylee and Amber to the car. He waited until Amber got in before turning to his wife to speak his mind.

"I don't know what the fuck is going on between you and that nigga, but this shit gon' turn out bad," Mekhi roared.

"What you mean you don't know what's going on between us? Ain't nothing going on with me and Zyrian, and I'm tired of you saying that shit," Rylee snapped.

"I came out here and saw you and that nigga staring each other down and you want me to believe it's nothing? That nigga is disrespectful as fuck and you don't make it no better. On God, Rylee, you can try to entertain Zyrian and his bullshit if you want to. That nigga gon' meet his maker and I'm knocking you the fuck out, straight up," Mekhi swore.

"Fuck you, Mekhi, with your insecure ass! You put your hands on me and Carolyn gon' bury your punk ass! Try me and see!" Rylee yelled as she got in her car and sped off, leaving him standing on the curb looking stupid. She couldn't believe that Mekhi had the nerve to threaten her, especially knowing how touchy the subject of domestic violence was with her. Rylee had to admit that the situation didn't look right and she understood why he was upset. But to threaten to kill Zyrian and put his hands on her was going too far.

"His stupid ass better not even think about looking for me tonight. I'm going by grandma and turning my phone off," Rylee vowed. She felt her anger rising with every word that she spoke. She needed her grandma now more than ever to help her stay calm.

"You want me to drive Rylee? You're kind of scaring me right now," Amber spoke up after a few minutes of silence. She had to do something before Rylee ended up killing them both. She was cutting corners on two wheels and had just ran her second red light in less than five minutes. She was clearly out of it, so Amber had to step in.

"I'm sorry Amber. Let me pull over right quick," Rylee obliged.

Amber got behind the wheel and drove with no known destination in mind. She ended up driving to City Park and stopping right near the amusement rides. She remembered her mother and Rylee's parents bringing them there when they were younger and they would stay for the entire day.

"This brings back so many memories." Amber smiled, trying to lighten the mood in the car.

"It sure does." Rylee smiled back.

Since Amber saw that her cousin had calmed down, she used that as an opportunity to say what was on her mind.

"I want to say something Rylee, but I don't want you to get upset. It's just my opinion, but I still want to voice it."

"What's up?" Rylee queried.

"I'm not taking sides here, but I can honestly see why your husband is mad. You might not notice, but I pay attention to everything. Zyrian can't keep his eyes to himself when you're around and he doesn't even try to hide it in front of Mekhi. I actually thought that the two of you were about to kiss out there a little while ago. A blind man can see that he wants you. And do you want to know what's even worse?" Amber questioned.

"What's that?" Rylee asked.

"A blind man can see that you want him too," Amber replied.

"God Amber," Rylee sighed dramatically. "This is so fucked up, but you're right. I'm attracted to him and I can't even lie. There's no way in hell that another man should be making my coochie cream like that."

"Ewe, that's gross." Amber frowned, causing them both to laugh at her silliness.

"I know, but that's how I feel. My emotions are all over the place right now. I'm mad with Mekhi. I want to fuck Zyrian. And I'm looking at these rides like I want to stay here for a while," Rylee rambled.

"Let's do it then," Amber suggested.

"You don't have to tell me twice," Rylee said as they hopped out of the car and walked deeper into the park. They got a wrist band for unlimited rides and ran around the park like two kids with no supervision.

Chapter 10

Mekhi paced back and forth from the living room to the bedroom with his phone glued to his ear. He'd been calling Rylee since the night before, but she had yet to answer. After his meeting at the biker's club, he came home preparing to apologize, but she wasn't there. He waited up all night for his wife to come back, but here it was Sunday evening and she had yet to return. She turned her phone off, so there was no way for him to get in touch with her. He'd been calling Zyra and Amber's phone for the past three hours and neither woman answered. Mekhi knew that the two of them knew where Rylee was, but they would never rat her out. He felt like he was losing his mind and the quietness of his empty house wasn't helping. He thought about driving around to find her, but he didn't want her to come home and not find him there. He was conflicted and he had a headache that just wouldn't go away.

When Mekhi's phone started ringing, he got excited until he realized that it was his work phone. When he saw that the call was restricted, he already knew that it was someone that he didn't want to talk to. He hit the ignore button and put the phone away. A few seconds later, a text message came through with a picture of a naked woman. Any other time, he would have been happy to see it, but he could care less right now. He quickly deleted the picture and sat down on the sofa. Although Rylee never touched his work phone, Mekhi still tried to be extra careful. Most of the numbers that called were restricted and he erased all the text messages and pictures right after they came through. The women who sent things through his phone did it with an app, so Rylee wouldn't be able to know who they were if she did see it. He could easily lie and say that it was a wrong number, if it ever came down to it.

"What!" Mekhi yelled when he finally answered the phone. It rung six times within three minutes and it was getting on his nerves.

"Did you forget about your daughter's nursery bill?" Shay yelled over the phone. "You haven't paid it in over a month and she can't go back until it's caught up!"

Mekhi blew out a breath of frustration. Rylee had his stress level on high and he didn't have time for anything else at the moment. He could care less about the bullshit that Shay was spitting.

"I don't know who the fuck you think I am, but you better keep it moving with all that squawking. I got too much on my plate as it is. I don't have time for the added theatrics," Mekhi replied.

"All I ask you to do is pay Mekhya's nursery bill so that I can go to work to keep a roof over her head. You can't even do that but, yet, you're on social media bragging about buying Rylee a ten-thousand-dollar purse and a Benz. Where they do that shit at Mekhi?"

"Bitch, don't worry about what I buy for my wife. What, you mad because a nigga don't do nothing for your washed-up ass? I'm trying to see why getting her nursery bill paid is my responsibility anyway. You're the one who wanted her, so you should take care of her. You forced me to be something that I didn't want to be. Fuck that nursery bill and fuck you too!" Mekhi snapped before hanging up the phone in her face.

He was already in a bad mood and Shay wasn't helping. She called back a few times, but Mekhi kept hitting the ignore button. When he got tired of doing that, he turned the phone off altogether. Shay and none of the other women he dealt with had his personal number and he wanted it to stay that way. If they couldn't get in touch with him on the work phone, then they didn't need to talk at all. Mekhi walked to his bedroom to put the phone on the charger right as the front door alarm sounded, letting him know that his wife had finally returned home. He was happy that she was back, but pissed that she had the audacity to stay out all night.

"So, that's how we're doing it now Rylee? You get mad at me and stay out all night?" Mekhi asked when she walked into their bedroom.

"It was either that or kill you in your sleep. You should be happy that I didn't come home," Rylee replied without a hint of anger in her voice.

She was upset the day before, but she had calmed down a lot since then. Talking to her grandmother helped, but going to church with her that morning really did the trick. It seemed as if the sermon spoke directly to her spirit and she needed to hear it.

"Look, I admit that I was wrong for what I said and I apologize. That still doesn't justify you sleeping away from home though Rylee. We're married and that's something that you just don't do. I get upset all the time, but I'm always home no later than midnight."

"Here you go with that midnight shit," Rylee complained.

"Unless we're out together, I don't see a reason why we should be out past midnight. Anything after that is the start of a brand-new day. Why is that a problem now? It was never a problem before."

"I never said it was a problem Mekhi. I'm sorry for staying out all night, but I just couldn't be around you for a while. For you to threaten to put your hands on me was just going too far. I stayed with my grandma last night to calm myself down and not do anything that I would regret later on," Rylee confessed.

"Rylee, I love you more than I love myself. You should know that I would never put my hands on you," Mekhi promised.

"Yeah, that's probably the same shit Cedric said to my sister before he put a bullet in her head."

"Seriously Rylee?" Mekhi asked incredulously. "You threaten me all the time, but you get all bent out of shape when I do the same thing to you. I'm not saying that it's right, but don't dish out what you can't take."

"But you, of all people, should know that certain subjects are touchy for me. Domestic violence and racism are two things that hit very close to home and you know that. Mad or not, you need to be mindful of what you say."

"You're right baby, but the same goes for you."

"Agreed," Rylee nodded.

"I just hate when you're mad at me. Come here," Mekhi said, holding his arms out for Rylee.

Rylee melted in her husband's embrace and the anger that she had for him the day before disappeared almost instantly. Mekhi could be an asshole at times, but he was a sweetheart underneath his arrogant exterior. When he let Rylee go and dropped to his knees in front of her, she already knew what time of day it was.

"Wait Mekhi, don't rip my underwear," Rylee whined when her husband reached under her dress and forcefully pulled at her lace boy cuts.

"Take all that shit off then," he replied.

Rylee assisted him with removing her clothes, before he picked her up and threw her in their huge king-sized bed.

"What are you doing?" Rylee asked when she saw him going into the drawer right next to their bed.

That was her toy box and Mekhi never went in there for anything. He didn't answer, but Rylee smiled when he came out with her fuzzy, leopard print handcuffs. Mekhi smiled as he cuffed both his wife's wrists to the headboard of the bed.

"You better not kick me either," he warned before he licked his lips and dove in head first. Rylee arched her back and prepared for the ride that her husband was about to take her on.

*****

"Hey baby," Rylee said when she answered the phone for her husband.

A few weeks had passed since she stayed away from home all night and things were back to normal with them. Mekhi was hell bent on having a baby and he was doing everything in his power to get Rylee pregnant. When her cycle came down a week ago, he was disappointed, but he was determined to make that her last one for a while. Rylee had been trying her best to avoid Zyrian and she was doing good so far. She still visited Zyra often, but she made it her business to go during the times that Zyrian wouldn't be home. She confessed to Zyra how she was feeling and her friend understood her dilemma. She would forewarn Rylee if her little brother was home or not, to make sure that they had minimal to no interaction with each other.

"Where are you, Rylee?" Mekhi asked his wife.

"I'm riding with Amber. We're about to go to Zyra's house."

Mekhi frowned, even though his wife couldn't see him. He promised her that he wouldn't trip over her being in Zyrian's presence, but that was easier said than done. Knowing that his wife was constantly around a man who he knew had feelings for her was messing with him mentally. He didn't know if Rylee was pretending or not, but she seemed to be oblivious to how Zyrian reacted to her. Mekhi often wondered if he openly flirted with his wife when he wasn't around. It got so bad that it was starting to consume his thoughts day and night.

"Mekhi," Rylee softly called out, shaking her husband from his trance.

"Yeah, I'm here," Mekhi answered.

"What did you need?" Rylee asked him.

"Oh, I'm at MJ's waiting for a delivery truck to get here and I need a favor. My mama needs eighty dollars to refill her prescriptions and I can't get to her right now. You think you can swing by and bring her a few dollars for me?" he asked, making Rylee roll her eyes up to the sky.

Carolyn was only fifty years old, but she was the laziest woman that Rylee had ever met. Sara was over seventy and got around better than she did. Carolyn always used her failing health as a reason why she didn't work, but Rylee knew that was bullshit. As long as she had Mekhi to take care of her, she never had a reason to lift a finger. Mekhi didn't pay attention, but Rylee noticed a few things about his mother. She was always asking for money for medicine, when she never used any of the medicine that she already had. Most of the bottles that lined her dresser were still half full and some had never been used. She claimed to have arthritis in her legs and hands, but that never stopped her from going places that she wanted to go. She also complained of having shortness of breath when she walked too far, yet she smoked a pack of cigarettes a day. Rylee didn't know what Carolyn needed money for, but it damn sure wasn't for medicine.

"Yeah, baby, I'm not too far from her. I'll swing over there right now," Rylee agreed before she hung up.

Amber knew the way to Carolyn's house since Rylee once lived there, and they were pulling up in the driveway about five minutes after. Both women got out of the car and walked right into Carolyn's house, just like always. Rylee looked around in disgust at how nasty the house was. The adults were lounging around like they always did, while Mekhi's nieces and nephews played with their toys. Clothes were all over the place and a few empty dishes littered the living room table and floor. Carolyn had an overflowing astray on the arm of the sofa that she accidentally knocked down the moment she saw Rylee walk in.

"Hey Rylee," she said, appearing to be nervous about her daughter-in-law's presence. "I didn't know that you were coming over today."

"Yeah, your son asked me to stop by and bring you some money. Whose baby?" she asked, referring to a little girl that she had never seen before. She knew all of Mena and Kendra's kids, but the little girl was a new face in the crowd. Rylee didn't miss the looks that passed between her in-laws, but she brushed it off.

"Oh, that's Kendrick's daughter. We're babysitting," Mena spoke up with a small smile.

"Kendrick!" Rylee shrieked in surprise.

"Yeah," Carolyn agreed.

"When did he have a baby and who is the mother? How old is she?" Rylee bombarded them with question after question. She and Kendrick ran into each other all the time, but he never mentioned that bit of information.

"It's some girl that he used to mess with. We just found out about her, but she's two," Mena answered.

"Oh, she looks just you and Kendra's girls. I can't wait to mess with him about this. He was the main one saying that he didn't want kids," Rylee laughed.

"Where's Mekhi?" Carolyn inquired.

"He's at MJ's waiting for the delivery truck," Rylee answered, handing her the eighty dollars that she requested.

"Thanks Rylee." Carolyn smiled.

"No problem, but I'll see y'all later. I need to get going," Rylee replied.

She and Amber were barely out of the door before Kendra started yelling. "Why the hell would you tell her that the baby belonged to Kendrick? You know she's going to ask him when they see each other again."

"What did you want me say? Oh Rylee, this is your step-daughter that you've never met and didn't know anything about," Mena replied sarcastically.

"Shit!" Carolyn hissed. "Mekhi is going to flip the hell out. I better call and tell him before Rylee does."

"I am so not for the bullshit that I know is coming," Kendra worried.

"Neither am I, but he has to know," Carolyn sighed as she picked up the phone to call her son.

*****

"Shit," Mekhi hissed. "Go all the way down Angel," he commanded as he sat at his desk, while Angel kneeled before him.

"I can't; it's too big," Angel mumbled with half of Mekhi's dick stuffed down her throat.

She was pissing him off with the constant complaining and he was ready to be done with her whining ass. She should have made good on finding another job because she damn sure wasn't worth much to him at the moment. He was busy checking in inventory when she propositioned him and, of course, he obliged. She was supposed to be cleaning tables and making sure the bar was restocked before they opened, but she had other plans. Since Mekhi had about an hour to kill, he decided to waste a little time on Angel. The manager on duty wouldn't be there for a while, so he wasn't worried about them getting caught.

"What the fuck did you beg me to let you come in here for then?" he yelled angrily.

Lately, every woman in his life was starting to get under his skin, with the exception of his wife. Rylee could take all of him to the back of her throat like a pro without gagging or flinching. She could go for hours and never got tired or complained. Usually, Mekhi would tap out before her and that was the only thing that he hated. Rylee wanted him to get some vitamins from his doctor that would prolong his erection, but he couldn't see that happening any time soon. Needless to say, Mekhi declined without giving it a second thought. Most women would have been thrilled to go for two hours straight, but that was just a warm up for Rylee. Mekhi considered his marriage to be perfect, with the exception of that one little flaw. Buck thought he was crazy when he confided in him, but he just didn't understand. Having his wife outdo him sexually messed with his self-esteem. He wanted Rylee to follow his lead, but he always ended up being led by her. Male pride was what Buck called it, but Mekhi didn't see it that way. He wanted to make his woman scream and not the other way around. In his mind, if his wife didn't make him feel like a king, there were plenty of other women that would.

"Let me make it up to you," Angel purred while standing to her feet.

Mekhi watched through hooded eyes as she lifted her short skater dress over her head, revealing the soft pink lace thong and matching bra that she wore underneath. Never taking his eyes off her short stacked frame, Mekhi reached into his desk drawer and pulled out a condom from the box that he kept there. As soon as he unwrapped it and attempted to slide it on, his personal phone started to ring.

"Don't just stand there," Mekhi snapped. "Come handle your business."

"You don't want to answer your phone?" Angel asked.

"Don't worry about that. Just do your thing," Mekhi instructed.

It wasn't the tone that was assigned to his wife, so everybody else could wait until he was done. No sooner than Angel sauntered over to him, Mekhi's phone started ringing again. This time, he picked it up to see who it was. When he saw his mother's number, he hit ignore and sent her to voicemail. By now Angel was completely naked, ready to slide her moistened middle onto Mekhi's awaiting erection.

"Mmmmm," she purred, as Mekhi filled her up like only he could. He didn't last as long as most of the other men that she'd been with, but he was damn good at what he did. So good that she ditched her previous plans of finding another job. She couldn't imagine not being with him like she was now and she wasn't ready to give it up.

"Ahhh fuck, damn Mekhi, slow down baby," Angel cried out in pleasure mixed with just the right amount of pain. She was on top, but Mekhi was drilling into her from down below. He had one of his hands around her neck while the other one pulled her hair. Hearing Angel's screams of pleasure was like a stroke to Mekhi's ego. It was the fuel that he needed to keep the fire inside of him going. He could care less if he was hurting her. Being with other women was for his pleasure, nothing more and nothing less. Lovemaking and feelings were for Rylee and no one else.

Once he got his nut, Angel would be a distant memory, just like all the others.

The sounds of their slapping skin and Angel's cries were all that could be heard until Mekhi's phone chimed, alerting him of a text message, followed by another ring. This time, the ringtone let him know that everything stopped when he heard it. It was his queen, the only woman who could make him move, even when he didn't want to.

"Shut up and stop moving," Mekhi instructed Angel right before he answered his phone.

"Are you busy, baby?" Rylee asked.

"No boo, what's up?" Mekhi lied, just like always.

"Oh, well, I'm headed to the mall with Amber and Zyra and I'm taking the black card," Rylee informed him. "What's my spending limit?"

"What do you mean what's your spending limit? You don't have a spending limit Rylee. Buy whatever you want."

"Okay, I'm just checking," she laughed. "Now don't freak out when the bill comes because you've been warned."

"I'll just do what I always do when it comes, and pay it. Get whatever you want and have fun. I love you, baby," he cooed with a cheesy smile plastered on his face.

Angel wanted to vomit once the words spilled from his lips. She felt like a damn fool for fucking him for free, while his wife was going on unlimited shopping sprees. The realization hit her like a ton of bricks, making Angel swiftly move from her place in his lap. Mekhi gave her a stern look, but she didn't care enough to stay. She was just applauding herself on her decision to stay; now, she felt stupid for not leaving sooner. Mekhi would never change and she had to come to that realization on her own.

"I love you too!" Rylee shouted before hanging up.

"The fuck is your problem?" Mekhi asked as he peeled off the condom and wrapped it up in the paper towels that sat on his desk. He stood up and adjusted his clothes like he didn't have a care in the world.

"I can't do this anymore Mekhi," Angel said as she choked back the tears that were starting to burn the back of her eyes.

"No problem. You can go ahead and get back to work then," he said in a dispassionate tone.

"No, I can't do any of it anymore. I can't continue to work here, knowing how I feel about you and knowing that you don't feel the same way about me. You constantly shit on me for your wife and I have to fault myself for that. For a whole year, I degraded myself by sleeping with you at your place of business or in my car. You never even cared enough about me to get a room. You've never taken me to dinner, a movie, nothing. Just straight fucking and nothing more. The only reason you gave me money at all was to abort the child that you helped to create. I can do better for myself and, starting today, I will," Angel said as he allowed the tears to flow freely down her face.

"Are you done?" Mekhi yawned like her speech had bored him.

"Definitely," Angel replied confidently.

"Good, you know where the door is; use it," he replied in a disinterested tone.

"I can't wait until Rylee finds out what kind of heartless bastard she's married to. She's too good for you and I hope she realizes that one day."

"You're saying a whole lot for a bitch who still got the smell of my dick on her breath," he smirked.

"Fuck you!" Angel wept as she made her way to the door.

"Been there, done that," Mekhi taunted while laughing uncontrollably.

"Let's see how funny it is when I tell your wife that we've been fucking for a year," Angel said, wiping the smile right off his face.

Angel was hurt, but she wasn't crazy. She had no intentions of talking to Rylee. Females did stuff like going to the wife all the time and they ended up looking stupid in the end. Aside from that, Angel never really wanted to hurt Rylee. She'd always treated her nicely and there was no bad blood between the two of them. Angel was wrong for messing with her husband, so she didn't have a reason to be mad. She just wanted to piss Mekhi off like he was doing to her, but she had obviously overstepped her boundaries. In a flash, Mekhi was standing in front of her with his hands wrapped tightly around her neck. Angel's eyes got wide once she realized that she had gone too far. He squeezed her neck with so much force that she saw the veins popping out of his forehead.

"Repeat that shit that you just said. Bitch, I'll kill you right now and I guarantee that they'll never find your body," Mekhi threatened in voice that sent chills through Angel's body.

Her eyes were watering and her breathing was becoming short and labored. She felt the life slipping from her body at the exact moment that Mekhi decided to let her go. The entire ordeal only lasted for a little over a minute, but it felt like a lifetime. Angel dropped to her knees and filled her lungs with as much air as she could. Saying that she was surprised by Mekhi's behavior would have been a lie. It wasn't the first time he'd put his hands on her, but she was determined to make it his last. She wasn't trying to stay in his office for another minute. As soon as her breathing regulated, she grabbed her purse and made a beeline for the door.

"Stupid bitch," Mekhi muttered as he sat at his desk and pulled his bottle of Cognac out of his personal liquor stash. He turned the bottle up to his mouth and closed his eyes, as the heat from the alcohol coated his chest. He reached for his phone to call his mother back, but decided to read the text messages first. Panic set in when he saw that Carolyn said that it was urgent and for him to call back right away. Mekhi dropped his cellphone on the desk and grabbed his office phone to make the call.

"What's going on?" he yelled when Mena answered the phone.

She put him on hold and Carolyn came to the phone a short time later. She started rambling as soon as she got on the phone, making Mekhi's heart take a nosedive in his chest. Things seemed to be going from bad to worse and the headaches just wouldn't let up. As if the problem with Angel wasn't enough, he now had to deal with some more bullshit. Both issues had the potential to break up his happy home and that was just something that he could not have.

Chapter 11

Mekhi arose bright and early the following morning to a big breakfast, courtesy of his beautiful wife. It was a Sunday and both of them had separate plans for the morning and, then, they were going to dinner and a movie later that evening. He and Rylee ate and talked like they always did before she left to go to church with her grandmother. Mekhi left soon after and headed straight to his mother's house. He was pissed and barely got two hours of sleep the previous night. He had to get to the bottom of a few things and he needed to do it quickly. He could have died a slow death when Carolyn told him that Rylee had seen Mekhya. Then, they took it a step further when they told his wife that the baby belonged to his brother, Kendrick. That was almost as bad as finding out that the baby was actually his.

Mekhi and Kendrick never did get along when they were growing up and not much had changed. Kendrick was a hater in every sense of the word. He was a fuck up who was jealous because his little brother had his shit together and he didn't. He was known to live off females and working was never an option. He and Rylee were cool and he probably would have loved to tell her who Mekhya's father really was. Mekhi hated that his brother had something to hold over his head. It was his own fault though. He'd forgotten to pay Mekhya's nursery bill for two months, leaving Shay stuck with finding a babysitter.

"Where is mama?" Mekhi asked his sister, Kendra, when he walked into his mother's home.

It was a mess, as usual. Three grown ass women in

a house and none of their lazy asses cleaned up. He turned up his nose in disgust when he saw all the toys and dirty clothes scattered about in the living room. The house had a stench coming from the kitchen and he soon found out why. Both sides of the sink and kitchen table were filled with dirty dishes that nobody bothered to clean. Mekhi went back to the living room and stood by the front door, waiting for his mother to come in. The stench of the kitchen had turned his stomach and he was ready to go.

"Hey son," Carolyn said when she walked in a few minutes later, followed by Mena and Mekhya.

"I need y'all to help me understand a few things. First of all, what is Mekhya even doing here? I don't recall asking nobody to pick her up," Mekhi said, looking around the room at everyone.

"Shay dropped her off a few days ago. She said that you hadn't been paying for her nursery bill and she needed a babysitter," Carolyn answered.

"Okay, but why is she here today? Shay works at the court house and they don't open on weekends," Mekhi informed them.

"I don't know son. I just try to stay on her good side to eliminate the unnecessary drama. She was talking about taking you to court for child support. I didn't want that to happen and run the risk of Rylee finding out."

"This is some straight bullshit!" Mekhi yelled. "Not only did Rylee see her, but now she's under the impression that she's Kendrick daughter. My wife was asking me why I didn't tell her that Kendrick had a baby and I didn't know what the fuck to say. What if she see that nigga and ask him about it? Then what?"

"We've already talked to Kendrick about it. He won't say anything to Rylee. I would rather her think he's the father than you. I didn't know that your wife was coming over. I would have had Mekhya in the room if I did," Carolyn promised.

"I didn't know that she was even here. You think I would have sent my wife over here if I did? Y'all let Shay spit that bullshit about child support, but that hoe ain't stupid!" Mekhi yelled.

"You need to call her and make some kind of arrangements. Maybe if you put Mekhya back in daycare, she'll back off," Kendra suggested.

"I'm not calling that bitch. I'm going to her house. Pack Mekhya's shit, I'm taking her back home. And y'all need to do something about this nasty ass house. I can be renting this bitch out to somebody who's going to take care of it if y'all can't," Mekhi fussed.

"We're about to clean up," Carolyn replied.

"You always say that, but it never happens. And why is there bags of trash sitting in the middle of the floor?" Mekhi asked, pointing to three big black garbage bags.

"That's not trash, that's Kendrick's stuff. That girl put him out again," Mena spoke up while going to retrieve Mekhya's belongings.

"Broke ass nigga," Mekhi mumbled under his breath.

Aside from a car, Kendrick didn't have shit to show for himself. He worked for six months at a construction site to buy it, but quit as soon as he had the car title in his hands. He always found a woman with her own house for him to lay up on, but it never did last long. Once his female companion saw that he was another bill and mouth to feed, they usually kicked him out. He always ran back home to his mother until he found his next victim, which usually didn't take very long.

"What's up baby daddy?" Kendrick smirked when he walked into the living room and saw his little brother.

"Nigga, you got a lot of jokes to say that you're depending on me to take care of your ass?" Mekhi snapped.

"Boy, you got me fucked up. You might take care of mama and the rest of them, but you don't do shit for me," Kendrick hissed.

"It's mighty funny you can say that when you're living in my house that I pay the bills in. I don't see nobody else footing the bill for nothing up in here."

"Don't get shit twisted. I'm here right now, but I won't be here long. You always trying to throw your money in a nigga face and shit. You up there now, but it's only a matter of time before you come back down here with the rest of us. Even balloons lose helium."

"Yeah, I know that's what you want to see happen, but it ain't. Even if I don't work for the next two years, I'm straight nigga," Mekhi bragged. "And unlike you, I'm smart with mine."

Mekhi didn't have as much as Kendrick thought he had, but he loved to piss his brother off. He and Rylee were financially comfortable, but they weren't rich. She still worked and saved all her money, so they had a little cushion if they needed it. Rylee had her own savings account that her checks went to, but Mekhi never asked her for anything. That was her play money, but he still made sure that he took care of all her needs.

"Kendrick, stop wishing bad luck on your brother. I don't know what's wrong with you," Carolyn said, interrupting Mekhi's thoughts.

"Still taking his side I see," Kendrick replied with a shake of his head.

That was nothing new though. Mekhi could do no wrong in their mother's eyes. She would go to her grave defending him, even if it meant going against her other kids.

"Here is her stuff. Come on Mekhya," Carolyn said while handing her son his daughter's bag.

Mekhya hung on to Carolyn's leg and looked at her father with tears in her eyes. She didn't see Mekhi as much as she saw the rest of his family and she was scared. It didn't help that he was yelling at her mother most of the time that she did see him.

"I hope she don't start that bullshit ass crying," Mekhi said with a frown. "I already got a headache."

Kendrick looked at his brother in disgust before calling out to his niece. "Come on lil mama," he said with his arms extended out to her. Mekhya ran and jumped in his arms, right before they walked out the front door with Mekhi following close behind.

"You got a car seat?" Kendrick asked Mekhi. He snickered when he saw the murderous look that his brother was giving him. "Oh shit, never mind."

"Just strap her in the back seat," Mekhi instructed.

No sooner than Kendrick sat her down, Mekhya started screaming to the top of her little lungs. She was pulling on his shirt, but he still managed to get her secured in her seat belt.

"Stop crying baby girl. Your daddy is going to bring you to see your mommy. You want to see your mommy?" Kendrick asked, trying to comfort her.

Mekhya nodded her head when he said what she wanted to hear. Kendrick wiped her face with the tail of his shirt and gave her a dollar, just like he always did. Mekhya was still sniffling, but she was no longer crying loudly. Mekhi was grateful for that much.

"Thanks man," Mekhi said to his brother.

"Thanks, my ass. I'll be at MJ's tonight and drinks are on you. I'm your daughter's daddy nigga, don't forget," Kendrick taunted.

Mekhi ignored him and backed out of the driveway. He sent Shay a text telling her that he was on his way. He didn't tell her that he had Mekhya because she probably wouldn't have opened the door for him if he did.

*****

Shay was just waking up when she heard someone bagging on her door like they were crazy. She had gone out the night before and it felt damn good. She hadn't been out in years and she was long overdue. Her mother agreed to keep her oldest daughters, and she left Mekhya with Carolyn over the weekend. She was about to pick her up that Friday when she got off, but her sister convinced her to go out for a night on the town the following day. Deidra tried to get her to go to MJ's, but she flat out refused. She wasn't trying to play games with Mekhi. Taking care of their daughter was all that she wanted from him.

"Who is it?" Shay yelled.

"Open the damn door!" Mekhi yelled back.

"Speaking of the devil himself," Shay muttered as she unlocked the door and pulled it open.

As soon as the door was opened, Mekhya came running in, followed by Mekhi. Shay was happy to see her baby girl, but she was wondering how she ended up with Mekhi. She didn't have to wonder for long when he opened his mouth to speak.

"Stop dropping her off at my mama's house without getting her permission first. My mama and my sisters are not obligated to keep her. And you don't even work weekends, so why was she still there?" Mekhi questioned.

"If you had paid her daycare bill, she wouldn't have been at your mama's house. I'm with Mekhya around the clock and I need a break sometimes too. It's not like I can drop her off to you, so Carolyn is the next best thing. It ain't like she clocking in at somebody's job anyway. All she do is sit inside and watch tv," Shay replied.

Mekhi dropped Mekhya's bag to the floor and got up in Shay's face. "Don't worry about what the fuck my mama do. She didn't sign up to be your personal babysitter. If you need a break, take her to your own mama. Last time I checked, her ass ain't have a job either."

"Just like your mama didn't sign up to be a babysitter, neither did mine. I'm putting your daughter off on everybody but you, and that's unfair. I didn't do this on my own Mekhi!" Shay yelled.

"But you did though. I gave you the money to get an abortion. You decided that you wanted to keep her without consulting me about it. Why should I be obligated to take care of something that I didn't want? You took away my choices and now you're pissed because I'm not there like you want me to be. As bad as I wanted a dog, I never got one because I didn't want to be responsible for it. That's the same way I felt about you having my baby."

"Are you seriously standing here comparing your daughter to a fucking dog?" Shay growled angrily. "So, I didn't get the abortion like you wanted me to, big fucking deal. She's here now Mekhi."

"Yeah, because of you. No matter what you say, all of this is still on you. When we first met, you told me yourself that you couldn't afford to have another baby, so why did you? I'll tell you why," Mekhi said as he asked then answered his own question. "You thought she was going to be your meal ticket. You saw how my wife was living and you wanted the same thing for yourself. But tell me, where is your sister and your cousins? They were the ones who convinced you to do it. Do they help you out with her?"

"They don't have to, she's not their daughter," Shay shot back.

"I'll take that as a no," Mekhi smirked.

"Look, all of this arguing is beside the point. Are you going to pay her daycare bill or not? I'm really getting tired of the back and forth. We can settle this like adults or we can get a judge to settle it for us. And honestly, we need to discuss you doing a little more for her than just daycare," Shay said seriously.

"You must be out of your fucking mind!" Mekhi objected.

"No, I'm actually coming to my senses. Rylee is not the only woman in your life who deserves nice things."

"I'm not giving you a fucking dime! As a matter of fact, I need the info for the nursery. I'm about to start paying them myself. I'll be damned if you use my money to take care of them other niggas' kids. You better fill out a missing person's report to find their asses to take care of their own kids," Mekhi replied angrily.

"Okay, but don't say I didn't give you a chance to do the right thing," Shay answered.

"I don't blame them niggas for bouncing on you. Don't nobody want your thirsty ass for a baby mama. Shit, you probably trapped them too," Mekhi said, hurting her feelings.

Shay was done talking. It was time to let her actions show more than her words ever could. She wrote down the info to Mekhya's daycare and handed it over to him right before he left. She slammed the door behind him and grabbed her iPad from her room. Shay was done playing games with Mekhi. She'd been letting him get by with doing the bare minimum for far too long. She was about to show him just how serious she was. Shit was definitely about to get real.

Chapter 12

Against his better judgement, Zyrian let Buck talk him into going on a double date with him and his girl, Asia. Of course, they didn't tell him that Asia's cousin, Renata, was who he was going on the date with. He was heated when he first got there, but he ended up having a good time. It turned out that Renata was just getting out of a bad relationship and that was why she came at Zyrian wrong the first time. She apologized to him and promised him a good time. He was happy to know that she'd kept her word. That was a little over two months ago and they were still kicking it regularly. The sex was still garbage, but he had other females who looked out for him with that.

"Congratulations boo, I'm so happy for you." Renata smiled brightly.

"Thanks Ma, I appreciate that," Zyrian replied.

It took a few months, but Zyrian was finally able to sell his house at full market value. The couple that made the purchase went to their closing earlier that day and he had the check deposited in his account soon after. He didn't have anything planned for the day, so he took Renata up on her offer to take him to lunch. They went to Deanie's Seafood in the French Quarters and Zyrian was enjoying himself.

"You want anything else?" Renata asked once she and Zyrian were done eating.

"Nah, I'm full. You can call for the check," he replied while rubbing his flat stomach.

He pulled out his wallet to take out some cash, but

Renata stopped him. "This is your celebration dinner, so it's my treat." She smiled sweetly.

Zyrian held his hands up in surrender and put his wallet back in his pocket. It was rare that you found a woman willing to foot the bill on anything, so her kind gesture was appreciated. Zyrian's father, Zach, used to always preach to him and his older brother, Junior, about selfish women. He always told them that they should always be the provider and never depend on their women to take care of them. But the flip side to that was to also make sure that they chose a woman who would have their backs if they ever needed it. He used to encourage them to test women by asking for something small and work their way up to bigger items.

Whenever Zyrian would get with a chick, he would start out doing everything in the beginning of the courtship. After a while, he would say that he wanted something but didn't have the money for it, hoping that they would offer to get it for him. He soon found out that a broke man, no matter how good he looked, was a huge turn off. Out of all the females that he had showed loved to when they went out, not one of them offered to show him the same, not that he really needed them to. He quickly got the picture and he started seeing things differently after that.

Whenever Zyrian spent money on a female he did so with the intention of getting something back at the end of the night and he always did. That was, until he met Dedy. She was the first woman to make him rethink his ways. Zyrian met her at a parade that his biker club was asked to ride in on Mardi Gras day. They kicked it on and on for a few months before they decided to make it official. By the time Zyrian met her, he was done with the whole testing females to see how they would react thing. Dedy's test was actually the real thing.

She and Zyrian were going to a party and they ran into the mall to get something to wear. As soon as they got in the mall, they went their separate ways, agreeing to meet up in a certain place when they were done. Everything was going good until Zyrian realized that he didn't have his wallet with him. He had everything picked out down to the socks, with not a penny or a credit card anywhere on him. When he called and told Dedy that they had to leave, she told him to stay where he was until she got there. Once she got to him, she didn't hesitate to pull out her debit card and pay for his entire purchase. It was a little over three hundred dollars and she didn't blink an eye when she did it. Dedy was only seventeen years old at the time, but she had a job working in a hair salon. She didn't do hair, but her brother's girlfriend let her wash hair and take appointments in her shop, just to keep money in her pockets. To say that her actions surprised Zyrian was an understatement. He was truly amazed, mainly because no one had ever come close to doing something like that for him. What was even crazier was that Dedy never asked to be re-paid. Of course, he gave her the money back with more added, but the point was that she never asked for it. It was then that he knew that she was the one. Or he thought she was at that time. Her true colors came out a few years later when he got locked up.

"You want to go catch a movie after this?" Renata asked, bringing Zyrian back to the present.

"That's cool, just let me run to the bathroom right quick," Zyrian said, standing to his feet.

He walked away towards the back of the restaurant to the where the bathrooms were located. After emptying his bladder, Zyrian washed and dried his hands before walking out.

"I thought that was you, but I just had to be sure," a familiar voice said from behind him.

When he turned around and came face to face with Dedy, he couldn't help the frown that appeared on his face. Zyrian looked her up and down and had to admit that she still looked good. Her hair had grown out a bit or maybe she was rocking a weave now. She was a little thicker than he remembered, but having a million kids did shit like that to you.

"Why would you need to be sure it's me? I thought you didn't have time for niggas in jail. Or at least that's what you told everybody."

"Really Zyrian? Since when did you start listening to other people? That was never your style."

"And it's still not my style. You showed me what it was, so obviously the rumors were on point."

"You don't think I thought about you while you were in there? That shit was just as hard on me as it was on you."

"I can tell by all the letters and visits I got from you," Zyrian remarked sarcastically.

"Oh, so that's why you're upset?" Dedy asked.

"Nah, I'm not upset at all. I should be thanking you if anything."

"Thanking me for what?" she questioned.

"For showing me that you weren't the one. Some niggas get in too deep before they realize that kind of stuff. You saved me a lot of time and money by showing me early on, and I appreciate you for that shit."

"Okay, now you're just trying to be funny. I know that you've moved on and everything. I saw you sitting over there with your lil girlfriend. I'm not trying to cause any trouble, I just wanted to say hello. We don't have to be together, but we can at least be friends. We've known each other too long not to." Dedy smiled.

"Girl, you ain't looking for no damn friends," Zyrian laughed. "You probably need help with them twenty kids you got at home. You still fine as fuck, but I'll pass."

"So, you're willing to pass on all of this," Dedy said as she made a sweeping gesture over her body.

"Hell yeah, I'm passing. I was only gone for five years and you had thirty kids during that short time. Your ass is fertile and I can't deal. I fuck you today and you'll be pregnant tomorrow. So, once again, I'll pass," Zyrian replied.

"Is me having kids that big of a deal Zyrian? You act like it's the end of the world or something."

"It's a not big deal for me at all. For your baby daddy, it might be, but I'm good. I'm just happy that I strapped up every time, so I don't have to deal with you like. But you be good Dedy, I'll see you around," Zyrian said as he walked away and went back to his table with his ex-girlfriend's eyes on him the entire time.

She felt stupid for even approaching him, but she couldn't let him leave without saying something. She knew that he wouldn't be too happy to see her, but he was downright insulting. Zyrian was always outspoken and nothing about that had changed. Dedy wished she would have made better decisions while he was in jail, but it was too late for what ifs now.

*****

"What's with the attitude now? I could have stayed my ass at home if I would have known that you would be acting like this!" Zyra yelled while putting her clothes back on.

She had stayed the night at the hotel with her friend, Jeremy. He had been begging her to spend some time with him, and she finally agreed. Now, she was wishing that she hadn't because he was seriously pissing her off. At first, he got mad because her girlfriend, Mica, kept calling. Zyra turned the ringer off and that seemed to satisfy him for a while. She even made sure that she was either outside or in the bathroom when she texted her back. He knew that she was with somebody, so Zyra didn't know what the problem was. Even Mica knew where she was and who she was with, but she didn't trip. Zyra was an open book. She was upfront and honest about her sexuality and a person could either take it or leave it. She was fine either way. She made it clear to whomever she came in contact with that she had infidelity issues. Some people called her confused, but she disagreed. She enjoyed the company of women and men, and she would never apologize to anyone for that.

"I don't have an attitude. I'm trying to see what's up with you," Jeremy replied after being quiet for so long.

"What do you mean what's up with me? If you want to know something, just ask. I don't have a reason to lie about anything."

"Okay, I have a question," Jeremy said, turning to face her.

"Shoot," Zyra encouraged.

"You have a huge two-story house that no one lives in but you and your brother. Why do we continue to come to hotels, instead of your house? You've been to my house several times and I've only seen yours in passing when I pick you up or drop you off. I just don't get it," Jeremy babbled.

"It's like you're smart, but then you're dumb at the same time. When we met eight months ago, I laid everything out for you. You knew that I didn't bring anyone to my house. I have a girlfriend who has never been there. I've been through a lot and I have trouble trusting people, and you knew that from day one. I've always given you the opportunity to walk away if my baggage was too much for you to carry. I'm fucked up in the head and it takes an equally fucked up person to be able to deal with me. I understand if you're not that person," Zyra answered.

Thanks to Tommy, Zyra had trust issues not only in her relationships, but with friendships as well. Everyone was surprised that she took to Rylee as fast as she did, but it was just something about her that drew Zyra in. Rylee was genuine and she never judged her or anyone else. She always told Zyra that whatever made her happy was what she should do. Her support meant more to her than she would ever know.

"Are you ready?" Jeremy asked, ready to leave.

Zyra was a beautiful person with a vibrant personality, but she wasn't the woman for him. He was thirty-two years old with no kids and he was ready to settle down and start a family. Zyra was a free spirit who lived each day like it was her last. They were on two different paths and it was time for them to go their separate ways. Jeremy knew that from the start, but he remained hopeful. The sex with Zyra was always new and exciting, and that's what kept him coming back. He could see himself loving her unconditionally, but she was right. Her baggage was too much for just one individual to carry.

"I'll be in the car," Zyra replied as she turned and walked out of the room. Jeremy took his time getting dressed, all the while thinking if leaving Zyra alone for good was what he really wanted to do. He would be lying to himself if he said that he wouldn't miss her, so he had a lot to think about. Once he was dressed, Jeremy made sure that he had his wallet and the key card for the room that they'd been occupying since the night before. When he walked out, he saw Zyra sitting in his car with her cellphone up to her ear, probably making plans with somebody else. Jeremy shook his head in defeat, as he walked to the front of the hotel to turn everything in to the front desk attendant. When Zyra saw him walking back to the car, she immediately ended her call and gave him her undivided attention.

"Look Jeremy," Zyra started as soon as he got into the car. "I don't want us to part on a bad note. I know that I'm a lot to take on and I'm surprised that you were able to hang in there with me as long as you did. With that being said, I understand if this is not what you want. Hell, I really can't say that I blame you. You're a good man with a heart of gold and I hope you find that forever ever with a woman who is just as good. Honestly, I know for a fact that that woman is not me."

As hard as it was to hear, Jeremy now knew what it was. He didn't have to struggle with if he was doing the right thing. Zyra had just confirmed that for him.

"Thanks Zyra." Jeremy smiled. "Most women would have probably strung this along, but I appreciate your honesty. That's rare these days."

"No thanks needed. Real in the only way I know how to be. I get it from my mama," Zyra joked.

"I see that," Jeremy laughed.

"So, where to now?" Zyra asked.

"Well, since this is officially our last date, how about we go grab something to eat? It's late and we haven't eaten since earlier," Jeremy suggested as he started the car. He kept talking about what he wanted to eat, even though Zyra was no longer paying him any attention.

"Wait Jeremy, don't pull off yet. Kill your headlights," Zyra instructed. Her attention was on the man who had just exited a room a few doors down from the one that they had just left out of. He was talking on his phone the entire time that he got into his car and pulled off.

"That lying dog!" Zyra screamed as the man drove away and disappeared from their line of vision.

"What's going on Zyra? Who was that?" Jeremy questioned.

"It's nobody that you know, but don't leave just yet. He didn't turn in a room key. Somebody else must be in there because I know he's not coming back," Zyra replied.

"Man Zyra, I work for the state. I'm not trying to be out here doing something that will cause me to lose my job. And I'm damn sure not about to sit out here and stalk no room that one of your niggas just came out of. That's not happening."

"He's not my..." Zyra started, but stopped midsentence when the door to the room swung open. Before Jeremy had a chance to open his mouth, Zyra was out of his car and charging towards the other woman.

"Shit!" Jeremy yelled as he unfastened his seatbelt and ran after her. It felt like he was moving in slow motion, as he watched Zyra deliver a blow to the woman's face that instantly dazed her and made her stagger. The woman was clearly caught off guard, but that didn't stop Zyra from stinging her face two more times with her closed fist. When the woman fell to the ground, Jeremy got to Zyra just in time before she finished her off with a kick.

"You nasty bitch! You're fucking my best friend's husband! Let me go!" Zyra screamed as she tried to break free from Jeremy's grasp. The other woman quickly stood to her feet and tried to come after her, but Jeremy wouldn't let her get close.

"Fuck you, Zyra! You had to catch me slipping in order to get one up on me. I told you from day one that Rylee is your friend. That bitch don't mean nothing to me!" Brandy yelled.

Seeing Zyra there was indeed a shock, but Brandy didn't feel bad. She'd been sleeping with Mekhi for the past two months and she didn't feel an ounce of guilt behind it. It wasn't intentional and she wasn't going to apologize for it. When she found out through Nicole that one of Mekhi's waitresses quit, she decided to put in for the position. Nicole was always bragging about how much she got in tips every night and Brandy wanted in. She tried her luck and went to MJ's one afternoon, hoping to get an interview.

Unfortunately, Mekhi wasn't interested in her working at his place of business, but he had another position in mind for her. One that she'd happily accepted without second-guessing. Brandy had always thought that Mekhi was cute and sexy as hell. Up until recently, she never would have imagined that he cheated on Rylee. He was like the ultimate husband and that was one of the reasons why Brandy was jealous of his wife. His sex was the truth and she wasn't giving that up for Zyra or nobody else.

"Let's square up then bitch!" Zyra yelled, pulling Brandy away from her trip down memory lane.

"I don't have time for this shit," Brandy replied. She knew that she couldn't win in a fight with Zyra and she was tired of wasting her time. Even if she wasn't caught off guard, Brandy was sure that she would have lost the brawl anyway. Her feelings were kind of hurt that Zyra kept referring to Rylee as her best friend. That was a title that she held not too long ago.

"I knew your ass wasn't right, but I tried to give you a pass," Zyra admitted.

"Are you sure you're not fucking him too? You're doing all of this behind the next bitch's husband. You seem suspect as hell right now," Brandy taunted with a chuckle.

"I don't even know why I'm surprised. Being a hoe is in your DNA, so you can't help it. At least your mama is getting paid to stand on Bourbon selling her ass. You do the shit for free!" Zyra yelled, hitting below the belt.

Brandy's smirk fell from her face just as quickly as it had appeared. She'd never confided in many people about her mother, and Zyra knew that it was a sore spot for her. If she never knew it before, she knew it now. Zyra valued Rylee's friendship far more than she valued hers. The gloves were off and she was ready to fight dirty too.

"At least this hoe can give her man some babies. You can't do shit with that dry rotted womb," Brandy laughed as she opened her car door and got in.

"Let me go, so I can kill that bitch!" Zyra screamed as she went crazy and started fighting Jeremy.

She wasn't surprised that Brandy came at her equally as hard with her harsh words. Zyra knew that she was wrong for bringing up her mother, but Brandy's words still cut like a knife.

"Ouch, fuck!" Jeremy yelped when Zyra bit the hand that was holding her back from getting to Brandy. At that point, he didn't care if both women killed each other. He was too busy trying to shake off the pain that he was experiencing. Zyra had her teeth marks in his hand and she even broke the skin.

"Get out of the car hoe!" Zyra screamed while kicking dents in her ex-friend's car door. Brandy was yelling obscenities the entire time, but she never got out of the car or rolled down the window. When she started backing out of her parking spot, Zyra picked up a huge slab of concrete and hauled it towards the fleeing vehicle. Brandy was able to speed away, but not before the boulder hit her car, knocking her side mirror completely off.

"Either you come on and let me bring you home, or you'll need to find another ride. This is some bullshit," Jeremy fussed as he walked back to his car mumbling under his breath. Like an obedient child, Zyra followed behind him and got back into the car. The drive to her house was silent and she was happy for that much. She didn't want to hear anything that Jeremy had to say. In fact, she was happy that this was their last interaction with one another.

*****

It was a little after midnight when Zyrian finally made his way inside. He knew that his sister was most likely home alone or still out with her male friend because no other car was there but hers. Once he opened the door and disarmed the alarm, Zyrian headed for the stairs until faint noises could be heard coming from the den area. Making his way down the hall, Zyrian soon found out that the voices were coming from the music that was softly playing. He pushed the door open and found Zyra deep in thought while nursing a glass of wine. He was happy that she was up because he wanted to tell her about his day.

"Man sis, you not gon' believe who I ran into today," Zyrian started before Zyra looked up at him with her bloodshot eyes.

"Who?" she asked in a voice that was barely above a whisper.

"Nah, fuck what I was saying. What's up with you?" Zyrian said, taking a seat next to her.

"I'm good baby brother. Just know that it's nothing that I can't handle."

"Crying is how you're handling it?"

"I'm not crying," Zyra protested.

"Not now, but you were. Are you going to tell me what happened or not? You already know that I'm not letting it go."

"It's Rylee," Zyra answered, making Zyrian's heart rate speed up momentarily.

Lately, Zyrian had only been seeing Rylee in passing and they hadn't had much communication. She still came to the house a lot, but he always seemed to miss her for some reason. It seemed like she was avoiding being in his presence, but he wasn't sure why. More than likely, it was Mekhi's doing, but Zyrian still didn't like it. He really missed Rylee and their daily banter. He missed her so much that he often found himself staring at the picture of her that he kept in his phone. It was one that he took of her the night of his party, but she wasn't aware of it. She was looking down at the bottom level of the bar when he got the full body shot. Rylee was camera ready, even when she wasn't. She only wore lip gloss most of the time, but her natural beauty couldn't be missed.

"What about Rylee?" Zyrian asked after a few minutes.

"I saw that bastard Mekhi coming out of a hotel room by the airport tonight. I made Jeremy wait a few minutes to see who he was in there with."

"Who was he there with?" Zyrian asked, although he had an idea. He assumed it was the same person that he saw him there with, until Zyra told him otherwise.

"It was Brandy," Zyra confirmed. "And I know that China probably knows about it because they've been together damn near every day lately."

"Brandy!" Zyrian yelled, not expecting her to say that name.

"Yeah and I tried to kill that nasty bitch with my bare hands. I'm just so confused right now Zyrian. Brandy was my friend, but Rylee is more like my sister. Even though I knew Brandy longer, there's no comparison between the two. I don't want to hurt Rylee, but I can't leave her in the dark. But, then again, I don't know how she's going to take it. What if she gets mad with me for telling her? That kind of shit happens all the time."

"You know your girl, Zee. You know that Rylee wouldn't get mad at you over some bullshit like that. But if you want my advice, I say keep it to yourself. Rylee and Mekhi are married. It would have been different if they weren't. That nigga is foul and it's only a matter of time before she finds out on her own."

"So, I'm supposed to betray my best friend to keep that nigga's secrets? I don't think so Zyrian. I'm telling her. I don't know how, but I am," Zyra said seriously.

"It ain't about keeping his secrets sis. I know you, Zyra; you'll never forgive yourself if you break up your girl's marriage."

"That's why I'm so confused. I don't want her to find out that I knew and didn't tell her. I need her to hear it from me. It'll break her heart if she hears it from somebody else."

"I know it's a hard decision to make, but I know you'll make the right one. If you need me to knock Mekhi's punk ass out, don't hesitate to ask," Zyrian said, making her smile.

Zyra could always count on her little brother to lighten the mood and she needed that more than ever. She was happy that Zyrian gave his input on the situation, but Zyra's mind was already made up. She was telling her girl everything that happened that night. She just hoped and prayed that the news didn't have a negative effect on their friendship.

Chapter 13

An entire week had passed since Zyra's run in with Brandy at the hotel and things were getting crazier by the day. Brandy told Mekhi what happened, and he had the nerve to call Zyra, trying to explain that it wasn't what she thought it was. He basically begged her to leave the situation alone, but Zyra was torn. He tried to make her feel guilty about possibly hurting Rylee and, admittedly, it worked for a little while. That was before Zyra's guilty conscience really started to kick in. She really felt like she was doing Rylee wrong and she decided that it was time to come clean. Zyra had gone so far as to confide in her mother about the situation. Of course, Glenda was just as upset, but she gave Zyra some very valuable information. She told Zyra to put herself in Rylee's place. Once she did, the decision was simple.

"Rylee Jameson, may I help you?" Rylee greeted when she answered her desk phone.

She'd been extremely busy since she walked in that morning and she was happy to finally be getting a break. Rylee's boss had been in and out of court all morning and one of the other attorney's secretaries was out sick. Rylee had been trying to do her work, as well as take messages for the other attorney. She had already worked well into her lunch break and she was starving.

"Hey boo, it's me," Zyra replied.

"Hey girl, what's up?" Rylee sighed loudly.

"Nothing much, but I can tell that you've been busy. This is my third time calling and your first time answering."

"It's been so crazy around here. I'm trying to do the work of two people and it's not easy. It's after two o'clock and I haven't even eaten lunch."

"Aww boo, you want me to swing by and bring you something? You know I don't mind," Zyra offered.

"Thanks sis, but I'm good. I'll just chew on these graham crackers until I get off. My hubby is taking me out to dinner tonight."

Rylee sounded so upbeat that Zyra was, once again, having second thoughts about what she was about to do. Her friend was happy and she had no right to take that away from her. She thought that maybe Zyrian was right and she should just let Mekhi hang himself. He was so sneaky with what he did; Zyra wondered when that would be. Mekhi even had her fooled into thinking that he was the ideal husband. Rylee didn't get treated like most women did when their husbands cheated on them. Mekhi still showered her with lots of love and attention. He wasn't one of the ones who changed up his routine and started acting differently. That's probably why he was able to get away with it. The more Zyra thought about it, the angrier she became. She was ready to get it over with and let Rylee know just what kind of snake she was married to.

"Well, what are you doing tomorrow? I was thinking that we could hook up once you get off. We can go happy hour at Gordon Biersch in Harrah's," Zyra offered.

"That sounds..." Rylee started before she was interrupted by the ringing of her cell phone. "Hold on Zyra, I need to take this call."

Zyra hung on the phone while chopping up seasoning to prepare the gravy steaks that Zyrian had begged her to cook. She loved having her little brother there, but he worked on her nerves sometimes. Zyrian was spoiled, but not in a bad way. He loved a good home-cooked meal and he was a bit of a neat freak. It was nothing that Zyra couldn't handle though. He spoiled her all the time too, so she didn't mind doing little things for him.

Zyrian was the reason that Zyra no longer had a job. She used to work for their local water company once she and Tommy separated, but Zyrian knew that she hated it. The money was great and that was the only reason why she stayed so long. He offered her a job working as a receptionist at his body shop, making the same amount that she made at her job. That was a no brainer for her and she quit her job the day after the offer was made. She reported to work bright and early the following Monday, ready to work. That was when she found out that Zyrian really didn't have any work for her to do. Their father kept up with the paperwork and all the appointments, leaving Zyra bored out of her mind most days. She complained to her little brother constantly and he finally told her the truth. He really didn't need her help at all, but he knew that she wouldn't let him give her money without feeling like she was working for it. Needless to say, that was Zyra's last day on the job and her last day working period. Even when Zyrian went to jail, he made sure that their father deposited money into her account every two weeks.

"Okay, I'm back; that was my doctor," Rylee announced when she came back to the line.

"Your doctor? Is everything alright?" Zyra questioned.

"Everything is great. That was my gynecologist. Happy hour sounds good, but no drinking for me right now," Rylee said with a hint of a smile in her voice.

"Are you pregnant?" Zyra asked.

"I don't know yet; that's why I had to take that call. My cycle is late and I've been calling to get an appointment since yesterday. They finally decided to call me back."

"Did you take a home test?" Zyra inquired.

"No, Mekhi said that they're not accurate. He wants us to go to my doctor. They're backed up with appointments, so I can't see him until next week."

"Well, I guess happy hour is out. Maybe we can go out to eat or something," Zyra offered.

There was no way in hell that she could tell her friend about Mekhi now. With the possibility of Rylee being pregnant, Zyra couldn't fathom giving her such bad news. She couldn't risk the health of her best friend's unborn child, no matter the reason.

"We can still go to happy hour. I'll eat while you drink," Rylee laughed.

"Sounds good to me. Invite Amber too, so I don't have to drink alone."

"Okay boo, we'll talk later. I need to answer this phone for the hundredth time today," Rylee replied before they ended the call.

Zyra went back to preparing her meal with more on her mind than she did before she called Rylee. Although they were married, she couldn't believe that Rylee would possibly be having Mekhi's baby. She really hated him with a passion, but she could never let her best friend know that. Zyra knew that it was going to be hard being in Mekhi's company, but she would do anything for her girl.

*****

"Excuse me, Mr. Jameson, but someone is at the front door asking for you," Frank, one of Mekhi's managers at MJ's, informed him.

"Who is it and what do they want? We're not even opened yet," Mekhi said, never looking up from his computer.

"I know, but he wouldn't tell me the reason for his visit. He just keeps asking for you," Frank replied with a shrug.

"Yeah okay, but whoever it is will have to wait until I'm done. I'll be there in a minute," Mekhi said dismissively.

Mekhi wasn't really doing anything important, but he didn't like to be rushed. He was the boss and whoever it was would have to wait until he was done sending his wife the edible arrangement that he was looking at. He loved to do little spontaneous things for Rylee and he would probably be doing it more often now that she was possibly pregnant. He was excited beyond words to know that he and his wife could possibly be having a baby. He was angry that Rylee couldn't get an appointment sooner than she did, but they had no choice. Her doctor was booked up and they had to wait it out. Rylee wanted to take an over the counter test, but Mekhi's mother told him that they were no good.

According to Carolyn, she had taken several tests while pregnant with him and they all said negative. She didn't find out she was pregnant until she went to the doctor almost five months later. As a result, she wasn't taking her prenatal vitamins like she was supposed to. Mekhi wasn't letting that happen to him and Rylee, so he passed on the home test. He wanted her doctor to confirm it and give them a prescription for vitamins right on the spot. And if Rylee was pregnant, he was ready for her to stop working. He wanted his wife to be spoiled throughout her entire pregnancy and stay home with their child until he or she was old enough for school. Having a baby with his wife was something that he always wanted and he couldn't wait to find out for sure. After sending Rylee's gift to her job, Mekhi shut down his computer and headed to the front of the bar. He didn't know who his visitor was, but he was soon about to find out.

"How can I help you?" Mekhi asked the casually dressed older man who stood on the other side of the door.

"Mekhi Jameson?" the gentleman asked.

"In the flesh," Mekhi replied

"You've been served," he said as he handed him a golden envelope and hurried away to his car.

"Served? Served with what?" Mekhi yelled after him.

It was too late because the man hopped in a tan Ford Taurus and sped out of MJ's parking lot. Dumbfounded, Mekhi walked back into his office and slammed the door behind him. He took his time opening the envelope and reading everything that it contained.

"That stupid bitch!" Mekhi yelled while slamming his fist on his desk.

He couldn't believe that Shay had actually sent him child support papers. She threatened to do it a million times, but she actually went through with it this time. Somebody had obviously put her up to it, but Mekhi was fuming. Although he was seeing red, all hope was not lost. The letter said that he had thirty days to either respond or make some type of payment arrangement with the child's mother. Mekhi had recently started getting money orders to pay for Mekhya's nursery, but it would kill him to actually have to put money in Shay's hand. He was sick over the fact that Shay would probably spend his hard-earned money on herself and her other kids. None of them were his responsibility and he didn't want them living comfortably off his funds. Once he calmed down. Mekhi grabbed the phone and decided to give Shay a call. He hadn't talked to her in a while and she didn't drop the baby off to Carolyn anymore, since he was paying for daycare once again.

"I guess the process server came to pay you a visit," Shay giggled when she answered the phone.

"Bitch, you think this shit in funny?" Mekhi snapped. "My wife could have been here and you pulled some shit like this."

"I don't give a damn who was there. I'm sick of this shit. If you don't want to take care of your daughter on your own, then I'll get the authorities to make you do it," Shay replied.

"I pay her daycare. What more do you want?"

"Her daycare is only four hundred dollars a month. She needs food, clothes, and everything in between. MJ's brings in enough money to meet all of your daughter's needs."

"Bitch, don't try to count my money. MJ's don't make as much as you think," Mekhi lied.

"Mekhi, you're not fooling anybody with that bullshit you're spitting. Y'all have parties booked every day for the next two months at one thousand dollars each, even on the weekdays. I did my homework, so don't try to play me, nigga. The way I see it is Mekhya should be good for at least a grand every month," Shay replied.

"A grand!" Mekhi yelled. "Bitch, you can suck a dick and die. I ain't giving you a grand every month for that lil girl."

"That lil girl is your daughter and that's the last bitch I'm gon' be. If you don't want to agree to my terms, then I'll see you in court."

"So, you want me to give you a grand on top of paying for her nursery? You got me fucked up for real. Ain't no judge in their right mind going to order me to pay fourteen hundred dollars a month for one kid."

"If he sees how much you're making, he might order you to pay more," Shay advised.

"Look Shay, I'm not trying to take this to court and have my wife find out about that lil girl."

"Mekhya! Her fucking name is Mekhya," Shay snapped.

"Whatever man. Since I'm already paying four hundred for the nursery, I'll give you six hundred more every month. That'll equal up to a grand every month. That's my first and only offer. Take it or leave it. Your rent is only five hundred, so that should be a big help to you," Mekhi reasoned.

Shay was quiet on the other end because she was thinking about his offer. She made pretty decent money on her job but, once the bills were paid, she didn't see much of it. Whatever she had left usually went to her girls or other household items. With six hundred extra dollars a month, she would be able to breathe a little easier. She knew that it was nothing compared to what she could be getting, but it was easier than going to court.

"Fine, but your first payment starts this month and on the first of every month after this one," Shay informed him.

"That's cool, but what do we do about this letter? I don't need these people to keep coming here even after we've come to an agreement."

"I'll have to call my case worker and tell her that we've worked something out. She'll close the case after that."

"And how do I know that you're really going to do that?" Mekhi questioned.

"There should be a case number at the top of your papers, along with a phone number. You can call and check on the status of the case at any time. I'll call her tomorrow and take care of that. But, in the meantime, when can I expect to have my money?" Shay asked.

"I'll send one of my people over there tomorrow," Mekhi replied.

"Why can't you bring it? You haven't seen your daughter in weeks. The only reason you called is because you got served with those papers."

"Don't let this child support shit go to your head. I'm only agreeing to this, so I don't have to go to court. You don't run nothing over this way, so don't start feeling yourself," Mekhi said angrily.

"All of that is irrelevant. Are you trying to see Mekhya or not?" Shay asked.

"Not," Mekhi said as he slammed the phone down in her ear.

Shay was one of the dumbest women that he'd ever met. There was no way in hell that any other woman would have agreed to the numbers that he'd just thrown out at her. Honestly, Mekhi was prepared to go much higher than that, but she was too eager to accept his first offer. Shay thought that she was in control of the situation, but she got played like the dummy she was. Knowing the kind of money that MJ's made every night, a grand a month was pocket change to Mekhi. He and Rylee spent more than that on shoes sometimes. Rylee had purses that cost ten times that much. Shay was desperate, so throwing her a few crumbs was easy.

That was one problem solved; now, he had to find a way to solve the other. Although Zyra hadn't told Rylee about him and Brandy yet, it didn't mean that she wouldn't. Mekhi tried to smooth things out with her, but she wasn't trying to hear it. It was a good sign that she hadn't opened her mouth yet, and Mekhi was praying that she never would.

Chapter 14

"Don't forget to tell your boss that you'll be late for work tomorrow," Mekhi said, right before he kissed Rylee and watched her back out of their driveway.

He rushed inside and got right into the shower, preparing to relax until it was time for him to leave. He had a busy day ahead of him, but the following day was free and clear. That would be the day that he and Rylee found out if they were expecting a baby or not. Mekhi was excited, but he had to put his feelings on the back burner for a while. He had to undergo an inspection at MJ's in a few hours and that was all that had consumed him for the past week. For the past few days, he and his employees had to make sure that everything at the bar was in working order and cleaned to perfection. If not, they risked failing the inspection and would have to close down temporarily. Usually, the state would give them thirty days to get everything in order or they would be closed down indefinitely until it was done. And if that wasn't bad enough, they even listed your establishment in the local newspaper, letting everyone know that your place of business had violations. Mekhi wasn't having that, especially since closing meant losing out on money. He worked around the clock and he made sure that his employees did the same. Rylee took the liberty of redecorating the bathrooms and that only added to the work that Mekhi and the workers had already done.

"Yeah Frank," Mekhi said, answering his ringing

work phone.

He was dripping wet, since he ran out of the shower to catch the phone after it rang three times back to back.

"We have a problem," Frank said, causing Mekhi to have an instant headache. That was not something that he needed to hear on that particular day. From Frank's panicked tone, Mekhi could tell that the news was indeed bad.

"What kind of problem? What's going on Frank?" Mekhi questioned.

"It's the grease trap in the kitchen. It must be clogged or something because there's grease all over the kitchen floor. It's going to be almost impossible for us to get it all cleaned up before the inspector gets here."

"What!" Mekhi's voice boomed angrily. "Did you call somebody to come and see about it? Please tell me that you didn't call me before doing that."

It was times like these that made Mekhi regret serving food at his bar. Although they made lots of money doing so, dealing with health inspections was something that he could do without.

"I've already called the number on the back of the manual. Somebody is on the way to repair it now. The problem is cleaning up this mess before our inspection. It's only three of us here right now," Frank replied.

"Fuck!" Mekhi yelled. "I need you to get on the phone and call everybody in to work right now! I don't give a damn if they're off or on vacation. Tell them to get their asses there now!"

Mekhi hung up the phone and put it back on the charger right next to his personal one. He rushed back into the bathroom, making a trail of water as he walked. Once he dried himself off, he got dressed in record time and ran out of the house like it was on fire. Instead of putting on his normal work attire, Mekhi threw on a pair of old sweats and a t-shirt. If things were as bad as Frank made it seem, then he would be putting in work right along with everybody else. He only prayed that Frank could round up all the employees because their presence was definitely needed.

*****

Rylee packed up her Louis Vuitton briefcase and shut down her computer. It was a little after noon and she was calling it a day.

"I hope you feel better Rylee. If you need some more time off, just let me know," Mr. Campbell said as he saw her to her car.

Rylee thanked him before she got into her car and headed home. She'd been trying to call Mekhi for twenty minutes, but he never answered. Rylee knew that he had an inspection at MJ's, so he was probably going crazy at the moment. She was praying that the bar passed because she knew how hard they worked to make sure it did. She also didn't want Mekhi to be hit with yet another bout of bad news. She was already about to give him some when he got home. She knew that he would be upset when she told him, but it wasn't the end of the world. After being over a week late, Rylee's cycle finally decided to make its grand appearance. She immediately called her doctor to cancel her appointment and see if she could speak to the on-call nurse. After talking for a few minutes, the nurse informed Rylee that it was normal for her body to go through different changes after getting off her birth control. She'd been on them for years and her body was trying to adjust. That also explained the terrible cramps that caused her to leave work early. Rylee never experienced cramps while she was on the pills. The pain that she was in at the moment made her want to get back on them.

"I need a hot shower and a bed," Rylee mumbled when she pulled up in her driveway.

When she walked inside the house, she immediately noticed that the alarm wasn't set. The door was locked and Mekhi's car was gone, so she knew that he wasn't home. He never forgot to set the alarm, so Rylee figured he'd left in a hurry. Once she went to their bedroom, her suspicions were confirmed when she saw both of his cellphones, as well as his wallet sitting on the nightstand next to their bed. The clothes that he planned to wear that day were still right where they were the night before. Rylee pulled out her phone and decided to give him a call at MJ's to see what was going on.

"MJ's, this is Frank," the manager said when he answered the phone. Rylee heard all the commotion in the background and she was regretting making the call. She knew that her husband was busy and she really didn't want to bother him.

"Hey Frank, this is Rylee. I was just calling to talk to Mekhi, but I'll call him back later. I can tell that y'all are busy getting ready for inspection."

"Hi Rylee," Frank greeted. "Yeah, it's been crazy around here. We had a little problem and Mr. Jameson had to come in early. He's not in the best mood right now."

"Enough said, don't even tell him I called Frank. I'll talk to him later on when he gets home. Good luck with everything," Rylee said before hanging up the phone.

After popping a few Advil's, Rylee grabbed a nightshirt and went straight to the shower. Once she was done, she made a big mug of hot tea and got into her big comfortable bed. She flipped through a few channels on the tv before she felt herself drifting off to sleep. Not even five minutes into her nap, Rylee's phone was ringing displaying Zyra's picture.

"Hey boo," Rylee answered groggily.

"Hey, I just called your job and they said you left sick. What's wrong? Do I need to come over there?" Zyra rambled.

"No girl, my cycle came down and these cramps are kicking my ass," Rylee chuckled.

"Oh, so I guess you don't need to take a pregnancy test anymore," Zyra acknowledged.

She felt bad, but she was secretly happy that Rylee wasn't pregnant. That would only further complicate things if she ever were to leave her husband. Knowing Mekhi, he would use the baby as an excuse for them to stay together. Rylee was big on family and everybody knew that.

"No, I've already cancelled my doctor's appointment. With the way I'm feeling now, I'm thinking about getting back on my pills. I've never experienced cramping before until now. This shit ain't a joke."

"That was the only good thing about me having a hysterectomy. I don't have to deal with that shit anymore," Zyra chuckled.

"Don't rub it in heifer," Rylee laughed.

"So, how did Mekhi take the news? I know you said that he was excited about everything."

"I didn't tell him yet. He had an inspection at MJ's and he's going crazy. We'll talk when he gets home," Rylee said, just as one of Mekhi's phones started to ring.

"What's that?" Zyra asked, referring to the music that was coming from the other phone.

"That's his phone. He left both of his phones and his wallet on the nightstand. He must have really been rushing to get out of here."

"Oh, well, what are you planning to do for the rest of the day? We can do happy hour now, since you know for sure that you can drink."

"Cool, but I need a nap first. What about five or six this evening? I'll pick you and Amber up if y'all want me to."

"Sounds like a plan. Get some rest and call me later," Zyra said before disconnecting the call.

She didn't have to tell Rylee twice. She turned over and was sleep as soon as her head hit the pillow. And just like before, the phone just wouldn't let her be great. It was like her phone and Mekhi's work phone was tag teaming, trying to see who could drive her crazy first. Rylee picked up her phone first to see that her grandmother and Amber had tried to call. They probably called her job just like Zyra did and were given the same message. She knew that her grandmother would worry, so she decided to call her first. That was before Mekhi's text message alert sounded off. Figuring that it was one of his off-duty employees, Rylee grabbed the phone to see who it was.

"What the fuck!" Rylee bellowed as she sat upright in the bed.

The picture of a woman's private area staring back at her almost made her vomit on her plush comforter set. Rylee's vision blurred with unshed tears as she read what the sender had written.

"We miss you" was all it said, but that wasn't the worst part. The colorful bed of roses tattoo right above her genital area that read *"MJ's honey pot"* was what did for Rylee. It was all the proof that she needed to know that her husband was cheating on her. The question was with whom. Rylee looked all through the phone, trying to get a face to go along with the picture, but that was the only thing that she saw. The sender must have used some kind of app or special technology to send it because the number showed up as all zeros. Apparently, Mekhi must have erased the previous conversations because the phone was empty. Rylee even went to the missed call log, but all the numbers were restricted. He was a slick bastard, but he had the right one. Rylee forwarded the picture to her phone and jumped

up from the bed. Through teary eyes, she threw on some clothes and grabbed her suitcase and overnight bag.

"Oh God!" Rylee screamed, as she fell to her knees in the middle of her huge walk-in closet. The reality of the situation hit her like a ton of bricks. Her husband was cheating on her but, for the life of her, she couldn't figure out why. She was a damn good wife, or at least she thought she was. She cooked, cleaned, and kept her house spotless. She fucked him into a coma most nights and sucked him until her jaws ached. She kept her figure tight and her wardrobe up to date. Obviously, that was all for nothing because she couldn't stop her husband from cheating on her.

With her knees pulled up to her chest, Rylee cried and rocked herself back and forth in a state of shock. Mekhi was her rock. He was everything to her outside of her family. He treated her like a queen and she adorned him with a crown just the same. True, they had their disagreements and arguments, but what couple didn't? At the end of the day, they were back at it like nothing had ever happened. Rylee couldn't figure out what she did so wrong, but it really didn't matter anymore. She was done. She'd never cheated on Mekhi and she refused to stay with him knowing that he couldn't give her the same respect. Once a cheater, always a cheater was what she was taught and she couldn't agree more. The fact that he was doing her wrong and she never suspected anything was enough for her to see just what kind of sneaky dog she was married to.

Rylee hated to doubt herself, but she couldn't help it. She had to be doing something wrong to make him stray. But, how could that have gone over her head? She wondered when it started and how long it had been going on. She never doubted Mekhi's faithfulness and he'd never given her a reason to. He was always accusing her of doing something wrong and, now, she knew why. He was the guilty one, but he tried to shift the blame on her. As much as Zyrian tried to get her to mess around with him, Rylee declined every time. She'd even gone so far as to stay away because she didn't want to be tempted by him. Obviously, her husband wasn't as strong willed and the proof was staring her right in the face. Rylee couldn't stop staring at the picture, even if she wanted to. The fact that the woman got her husband's initials tattooed on her let Rylee know that the affair had to be an ongoing thing and it didn't just start. Although she couldn't be mad at the other woman, she still wanted to know who she was.

Two hours later, Rylee was still in the same spot that she was in before. Her eyes were swollen and burning from all the crying that she had done. Finally gaining the strength to get up, Rylee started throwing items in her bags. She had so many clothes and shoes that it would probably take an entire day to have everything moved. She started with the basic items, like work clothes and most of her hygiene items. She would have Zyra and her cousins help her come for everything later. She would probably have to buy a few things, but that wouldn't be a problem. She had a lot to figure out, but one thing she knew for sure. Her marriage was over and there was no doubt in her mind about that.

Chapter 15

It was after three that afternoon when Mekhi finally left the bar. He was in such a hurry when he left that morning, he hadn't taken any of his cellphones or his wallet. He was happy that he didn't get stopped because he was damn near doing one hundred trying to get to his bar. Thankfully, the problem at MJ's was fixed and they were able to get the kitchen spotless before the inspector came. He was in full panic mode earlier that day, but everything worked out fine. MJ's passed with flying colors and Mekhi was finally able to exhale. Mostly all his employees came in to help and he made a note to do something special for them soon. Mekhi was an asshole most of the time, but he had a soft heart when he wanted to. He was tired, but he wanted to be back at MJ's later that night when they opened. He didn't plan on staying long because he wanted to spend some time with his wife.

Pulling up to his house, Mekhi was surprised to see Rylee's car in the driveway. She wasn't due home for another two hours and she rarely left work early. He pulled his car right next to hers and made his way inside. He heard Rylee on the phone and it almost sounded like she was crying. When he walked into their bedroom, Mekhi's heart dropped at the sight before him. Rylee's swollen red eyes and tear stained face was nothing compared to the mess that she'd made of their room. She had her clothes thrown all over the place, while she stuffed some more into huge black garbage bags.

"What the hell is going on Rylee?" Mekhi inquired

when he walked up on her.

"Don't say shit to me. The next time you see me will be in divorce court," she promised.

"Divorce court!" he yelled in shock. "What the fuck are you talking about?"

"This is what I'm talking about nigga!" Rylee yelled as she shoved his work phone in his face.

Two other text messages came through with the same picture but, this time, the person wanted to know when he would be free to meet up. She even mentioned them hooking up in his office at MJ's again. That was all the confirmation that she needed. It took everything in Rylee not to reply. As far as she was concerned, her problem wasn't with the other woman. She wasn't doing anything more than what Mekhi was allowing. Rylee had forgotten all about Zyra being on the phone. She was too busy trying to see Mekhi's reaction to the picture that she'd shown him. He tried to play it cool, but Ryle could see the sweat forming on his brows.

"Who is that and why are you showing it to me?" Mekhi asked like he was shocked.

"Okay Mekhi, if that's the game that you wanna play, I'll play along. You're a fucking liar and a cheater. As far as I'm concerned, this marriage is over. I'm happy that I'm not pregnant by your dog ass. Maybe my next man will appreciate me and I can give him some babies," Rylee snapped. Her hurt had turned in rage and she was done crying for now.

"You must be out of you fucking mind if you think you're leaving me behind some bullshit that I don't know nothing about. Somebody probably sent that to the wrong number and you're blowing up on me over it."

"I figured you'd say that. I guess the person that she wanted to send it to has your initials too, huh. And I guess they also have a business called MJ's. You're busted, plain and simple. Do us both a favor and keep it real. It's over so, no matter what you say, my mind is already made up."

"You ain't going nowhere!" Mekhi yelled as he grabbed one of her bags and dumped the clothes out. "Somebody is fucking with you and you're dumb enough to take the bait. We're married and we're going to sit down and talk about this like adults."

Mekhi tried his best to sound unaffected, but his heart was beating out of his chest. He was indeed busted, but he would never admit that to his wife. The thought of Rylee leaving him was something that he never contemplated. She was his whole world, but he didn't think about any of that when he was doing wrong.

"I'm dumb?" Rylee asked while pointing to herself. "No, nigga, you're the dummy if you think I believe that shit that's coming out of your mouth. Give me my shit and get out of my way."

"I said you ain't going nowhere!" Mekhi yelled while pulling her by her long ponytail.

"Nigga, you must have lost your damn mind!" Rylee screamed as she turned around and started swinging on him. She dropped the phone, so she never heard Zyra yelling that she was on her way over. She had already asked Buck to go over there, just in case something popped off. She knew that Mekhi wouldn't take Rylee's leaving too well and she was prepared.

"Chill out Rylee. I'm trying to keep from hitting you, but you better calm the fuck down!" Mekhi yelled as he tried to block some of the punches that she threw his way.

"Let me go!" Rylee yelled when he grabbed her arms and held them to her side.

"Baby, please calm down and let's talk about this," Mekhi begged.

"We can talk, but only if you're planning on telling me the truth," Rylee answered out of breath.

Mekhi contemplated his next move, but he really didn't have a choice. He had to come clean, but he wouldn't dare reveal everything.

"I swear, I'll tell you everything that you want to know," Mekhi lied with a straight face. "But you have to promise me that you won't leave me when I do."

"Okay, I promise," Rylee agreed as he let her arms go. "Who is she and how long have you been messing around with her?"

"You don't know her, but we met at MJ's," Mekhi said as he looked at the tile underneath his feet.

Rylee knew that he was lying because he could never look her in the face when he did. "How long?" Rylee repeated the question that she really wanted answered.

"A few months," Mekhi said as he continued to study the floor.

"Do you love her?" Rylee asked as a few stray tears escaped her eyes.

Mekhi's gaze landed on her as soon as the words left her mouth. "What? Baby, no, I don't love her. I've never loved another woman besides you."

"Obviously not enough though, right?"

"Rylee, please don't do that. Don't doubt my love for you. I fucked up, but I swear I'll do anything that I can to make it right. Just tell me what I have to do," Mekhi pleaded with tears in his eyes.

"Just sign the divorce papers when they come," Rylee urged.

"You just promised me that you wouldn't leave."

"Yeah, just like you promised to always be faithful. I guess we're both liars," Rylee said, right as the doorbell rang.

She raced to the front of the house with Mekhi right on her heels. She swung the door open and Zyra came strolling right on in.

"Who the fuck invited you to come in?" Mekhi snapped.

"Fuck off Mekhi. I'm coming to check on my friend. You need help with your bags Rylee?" Zyra asked.

"Nah, she ain't going nowhere, but you need to go."

"I invited her here and she's not leaving without me. Come on, I have a few bags packed already," Rylee said to Zyra.

Mekhi stepped up and blocked them from going into their bedroom. "You need to tell your girl to keep it moving. We need to talk."

"We've already talked and I'm done. Let me get my shit and I'm out of here. You can do whatever you want once I'm gone. You don't have to sneak around anymore," Rylee assured him.

"You need me to call my cousins, Rylee?" Zyra offered.

"Am I supposed to be scared Zyra?" Mekhi asked. "You can call whoever the fuck you want. Nobody ain't scared of your cousins. Them niggas ain't the only ones with guns."

"Nah, but we ain't scared to use our shit," Grim replied as he and Buck walked through the opened front door.

Mekhi wanted to piss in his pants, but he kept a straight face. Zyra must have already made some calls before she came to their house, and he wasn't prepared for the trouble that would come with it. He wasn't a killer, but Grim and Snake's résumés proved that they were.

"What's going on bruh?" Buck asked his boy.

"Whatever is going on is between me and my wife. I don't even know why y'all are here," Mekhi spoke up.

"Damn Mekhi, it's like that?" Buck asked, sounding offended.

"Nah man, but this is a personal issue that we need to resolve on our own. You know we're cool Buck, but this don't have nothing to do with nobody else but me and Rylee," Mekhi reasoned.

"Alright then, man. I respect that. Let's go Zyra," Buck said to his cousin.

"No, not unless Rylee wants me to leave. Are you staying Rylee? It's okay if you are, but I want to know that you're going to be alright," Zyra asked.

"She's good," Mekhi snapped in irritation.

"Nigga, your name ain't Rylee and you better watch your tone with my cousin. I would hate to do you dirty in your own house, but I will!" Grim yelled.

"Chill out man. We're wrong for even being in this man's house like this, so calm down," Buck reasoned. "What's up Rylee? You good or what?"

"No, I'm leaving," Rylee said, breaking Mekhi's heart into a million pieces.

"Don't do this Rylee. Can we just sit down and talk about it?" Mekhi begged.

"Maybe in a few days, but I can't talk to you right now," Rylee replied.

"What about your doctor's appointment tomorrow?"

"I cancelled it. My cycle came on this morning. That's why I came home early and that's how you got busted."

"Where are you going Rylee?" Mekhi asked.

"I don't know yet."

"Can you please go by your grandmother and not to her house?" Mekhi pleaded while pointing at Zyra.

He would go crazy for sure if he knew that his wife was sleeping under the same roof as Zyrian. He'd done his share of dirt, but he couldn't wrap his mind around Rylee being with anybody else.

"Okay," Rylee agreed.

Mekhi stepped aside and allowed his wife and her friend to grab some of the clothes that she'd already packed up. Once they were gone, he cleaned up the mess that Rylee had made and went to take a shower. He was supposed to be going back to MJ's for a while, but he really wasn't in the mood to do much of nothing. The first thing he did want to do was call the dumb bitch who sent the picture to his phone though. It wasn't her fault that he got caught cheating, but some of blame was being placed on her anyway. God forbid if Rylee ever found out who it was. She would be divorcing him for sure if she did.

*****

"How you feeling boo?" Zyra asked Rylee.

"Stupid," Rylee mumbled as she stared at the wall and wiped the tears from her eyes.

"You are not stupid Rylee. Stop beating yourself up for something that wasn't your fault."

"But, why didn't I know Zyra? How could my husband have a relationship with another woman and I had no idea? I mean, not even a clue that he was cheating on me. That shit even sounds crazy."

"I don't know honey, but don't be too hard on yourself. It happens to the best of us. Look at my situation. At least Mekhi didn't bring the bitch home to you like Tommy did me."

"I would have killed both of their asses and pleaded insane," Rylee said, making her friend laugh at the serious look on her face.

"You're crazy enough to do some shit like that too. But seriously, Rylee, you know that you can stay here as long as you like. I hate living in this big ass house by myself. That's why I'm happy that Zyrian moved in with me."

"Where is he anyway?" Rylee asked, referring to Zyrian.

"He's probably out with Renata somewhere," Zyra replied.

Rylee didn't know why, but she felt a little jealously trying to creep in when Zyra mentioned her brother being with another woman. She hadn't seen too much of Zyrian lately, but she knew that would all change soon. Even though she promised Mekhi that she was going to her grandmother's, Zyra's house was the first place that she went to. She didn't give a damn about how he felt. He didn't have any say in what she did anymore.

"Listen, I need to tell you something and I hope that you're not mad at me once I tell you," Zyra announced.

Rylee noted the nervous look on Zyra's face. She wasn't sure if she was ready for whatever she had to say, but curiosity got the best of her.

"I'm listening," Rylee answered.

"You remember when Jeremy and I stayed the night at the hotel week before last?" Zyra asked.

"Yeah," Rylee replied while urging her to continue talking.

"Well, right before we left, I saw Mekhi coming out of one of the rooms. I didn't say anything to him, but I waited to see if somebody else would come out after him."

"And?" Rylee asked as she held her breath, preparing for the answer.

"It was Brandy," Zyra confessed. "The day that I called your job asking you to meet me for drinks is when I planned to tell you about it. But when you told me that you could possibly be pregnant, I couldn't do it. I'm sorry for keeping it from you, but I was torn."

She expected Rylee to yell or even cry, but she just sat there stone faced, as if she was traumatized.

"Did you hear me, Rylee?" Zyra said, trying to break her friend from the shock that she seemed to be in.

"Yeah, I heard you," Rylee murmured. "I'm not mad at you, Zyra. I'm not even surprised about Brandy. She made it clear from day one that nobody's man was off limits. I guess that warning was meant for me too. She and I were never friends, so that made Mekhi fair game to her."

Rylee knew for a fact that the picture in Mekhi's phone wasn't Brandy. The woman in the picture had a caramel complexion, while Brandy was the color of dark milk chocolate.

"Well, I'm done with her. China and I had it out too because she was taking Brandy's side. I'm sure she knew what was going on and she's just as foul. Cousin or not, she can get the business too."

"It's all good. I'm hurting now, but I won't be hurt forever. I just feel like a damn fool for letting this go over my head for God knows how long."

"You are not a fool and I wish you would stop saying that. It's life and it happens all the time. You're not the first woman that this has happened to and you damn sure won't be the last. Just know that I'm here for you, no matter what you decide to do. Even if you want to go back."

"There is no going back Zyra. I want a divorce and that's all there is to it," Rylee swore.

"You're just mad right now because it's still fresh. You'll feel better in a few days."

"Correction, I'm not mad; I'm enraged. And I won't feel better until I no longer have his last name. I grew up in a two-parent home just like you did, so I know how a man is supposed to treat a woman. I watched my father treat my mother like a queen up until she took her last breath. I refuse to settle for anything less than that."

"I agree, but I don't want you to give up on love. Don't let what Mekhi did make you bitter," Zyra warned.

"It won't make me bitter. If anything, it'll make me better. And I'm not giving up on love. I'm just giving up on loving my husband. He doesn't deserve it."

"The true words of a bad bitch," Zyra said, making Rylee laugh.

*****

Zyrian rolled inside around two in the morning. He got excited when he pulled up and saw Rylee's car in the driveway. He waked through the front door and stopped in his tracks when he saw all the bags in the living room. He took the stairs two at a time until he got to Zyra's room. When he saw that she wasn't in there, he walked down the hall, following the laughter that was coming from another room. He opened the door and smiled at Rylee and Zyra, who were sprawled out across the bed eating from a huge bucket of chocolate ice cream. Rylee's red, swollen eyes were the first thing that he noticed upon entering the room.

"What's wrong with my wifey? Who do I need to fuck up for messing with you?" Zyrian asked as he took the spoon from Rylee's hand and ate the ice cream that she'd just scooped out of the bucket.

"Mekhi Jameson is his name and I have the address if you need it," Rylee joked.

"Nah, but seriously, what happened?" Zyrian inquired.

"Where do I start? Well, first off, my husband is a man whore who played me to the left for God knows how long. I have no house because I refuse to go back to the one that I shared with him. I have cramps that won't go away and, instead of sharing my ice cream with one person, I now have two extra mouths to feed. Plus, I'm about to be divorced on top of all of that. So, that just about sums up my life. Hopefully, I didn't leave anything out," Rylee sighed.

"Damn, tell me how you really feel," Zyrian laughed.

"Stop saying that you don't have a house. You can stay here as long as you want to. It's not like we don't have the room," Zyra responded.

"I know, I'm just trying to laugh to keep from crying again," Rylee chuckled.

"You better not let me see you crying over that nigga. He ain't even worth your tears. I know that's your husband and all, but fuck him!" Zyrian snapped.

"You always know just what to say to make me feel better," Rylee said sarcastically.

"I'm serious though, Rylee. You got too much going for yourself to let any man bring you down. His loss is the next man's gain," Zyrian said, hoping that she caught the hidden message behind his words.

Zyrian was happy as hell that Mekhi finally did something to mess up. He knew that he was wrong for feeling that way, but he couldn't help it. Of course, Rylee wouldn't be ready to start up something else so soon, but he had nothing but time on his hands. She was worth waiting for and he would do it patiently. Playing the friend role was good for now but, in due time, it would develop into something more. He was about to show Mekhi and everybody else how a queen was supposed to be treated. Rylee smiled and thanked him before he got up to leave. His words made her feel better, but she didn't know for how long. For years, Mekhi was all that she knew. She knew that she would get over him eventually, but it wasn't going to be easy.

Chapter 16

Two whole weeks had passed since Rylee left home, and Mekhi was losing it. He'd been calling her phone non-stop until she eventually blocked him from calling altogether. She swore to him that they would discuss everything at a later date, but that turned out to be a lie. She also promised that she wouldn't go stay with Zyra, but that's exactly where she went. Mekhi now knew that she basically told him whatever he wanted to hear, in order to get away from him with no problems. The thought of his wife actually leaving him for good was making him crazy. And the thought of her being under the same roof as Zyrian was enough to make him want to commit a crime. Then, as if things weren't already bad enough, Zyra opened her big ass mouth and told Rylee about him and Brandy. Rylee wouldn't tell him how she found out, but she didn't have to. He knew without a doubt that Zyra was the guilty one.

"Man, you need to chill out with all that drinking. That's all you've been doing lately," Buck said as he and Mekhi sat at the bar at MJ's.

The bar wasn't opened just yet and they were the only two in there for now. This was actually Mekhi's first time going back since the night Rylee left. He'd been in a deep depression and wanted to be left alone. Frank and his other managers made sure everything ran smoothly because he wasn't in the mood.

"Bruh, I'm stressed the fuck out!" Mekhi yelled. "Rylee is still on that bullshit, talking about a divorce. I swear, I see why ole boy did what he did to her sister. This shit is messing with me mentally."

"That's fucked up Mekhi. You wrong for even saying some shit like that," Buck said in disgust.

"Man, I love Rylee more than I love myself. You know I wouldn't do nothing to hurt her."

"What do you think you were doing when you were cheating on her? That shit hurt her too. That girl is fucked up over this man. You probably lost a good woman, all because of these bum bitches that you be messing with. And then you got hoes sending pictures to your phone, knowing that your wife might see it," Buck argued.

"Rylee never touched my work phone before. The only reason she touched it that time was because I wasn't there to get it myself."

"But, that's still not an excuse," Buck said, continually arguing his point.

"I know it's not an excuse. I'm done bruh; on God, I'm done with all of that other shit. I just need to get back right with my wife."

"You better hope it's not too late," Buck warned.

"Whose side are you on? You talking like you don't want me to get back right with her. What, you trying to make sure she's available for your cousin?" Mekhi accused, giving him the side eye.

"Nigga, don't try to come at me sideways on no stupid shit like that. Zyrian got a girl, so he ain't checking for Rylee and nobody else right now. You fucked up and now you're mad because you got caught. You knew that hoe was off limits, but you just had to go there. You need to be happy that Rylee don't know who it is. And your ass better be lucky that she didn't find out about that lil girl that you've been hiding."

"I know I messed up, but I'm trying to fix it if she'll let me."

"A broken promise is one of the hardest things to fix. You need to think on that. I'm out," Buck said as he got up and walked out of the front door.

Mekhi had a lot on his mind already and Buck just gave him even more to think about. He was right; he did break his promises to his wife. The only thing he had to do was be faithful and he couldn't even do that. He just needed another chance to get it right. Rylee wasn't even taking his calls, so he couldn't even plead his case. He didn't want to show up at Zyra's house or her job, but she wasn't giving him any other choice. He decided to give her a few more days and then he was going to get his wife back.

*****

"You know you don't have to babysit me every weekend Zyrian. I'll be fine," Rylee said.

"What would you look like going to the movies all by yourself? I don't mind hanging with you while your best friend is out being a hoe," Zyrian laughed

"Don't call my friend a hoe. She's just doing her. Maybe I should have been more like her and I wouldn't have gotten messed over."

"Nah, that's not your style. You're a good girl, so being a hoe wouldn't have worked for you."

"Yeah, but look at what being a good girl got me," Rylee challenged.

"Why do you keep blaming yourself for Mekhi cheating on you? That nigga was foul, but that ain't have nothing to do with you," Zyrian assured her.

"I know, but I just can't help but think that it was something that I wasn't doing to make him look elsewhere. I know it sounds cliché, but that's how I feel," Rylee said as she drove to their destination.

When they pulled up to the movie theater, Rylee got out, walked up to the automated ticket machine, and got two tickets for her and Zyrian to see *Creed*. After getting them some snacks, Rylee and Zyrian found some decent seats and enjoyed the movie. Once they were done, they drove around while talking about nothing in particular. Zyrian showed her the house that he'd just sold and took her to the area that he wanted to get another house in.

"You wanna go grab something to eat before we go in?" Rylee asked.

"That's cool," Zyrian replied.

He and Rylee ended up at New Orleans Food and Spirits, enjoying a huge grilled shrimp salad. Their conversation flowed effortlessly and Zyrian loved that about Rylee. She could talk about anything from sports to politics and keep the conversation entertaining.

"Hey Rylee," a slightly familiar voice greeted.

Rylee smiled when she looked up and saw Angel standing at their table. She wasn't the waitress who took their order, so Rylee figured that she was probably just now coming to work. Despite the minor attitude that Angel seemed to have occasionally, she and Rylee were cool. Rylee knew that she was no longer working at MJ's, but Mekhi never told her why.

"Hey Angel, I didn't know that you worked here now," Rylee spoke back, just as she sat their bill on the table.

"I got it. You already paid for everything at the movies," Zyrian offered when he saw Rylee reaching for it.

Angel looked back and forth between the two of them, trying to figure out what was going on. Although Mekhi did his thing regularly, Angel never took Rylee for the cheating type. She couldn't figure out where she knew the man from, but she could definitely see why he had Rylee's attention. He was very attractive to say the least.

"No," Rylee said, snatching it from his hand. "You're doing me a favor by keeping me company. It's my treat."

Zyrian tried to hide his smile, but it was hard. Beautiful and selfless, Rylee was definitely a keeper. She handed Angel some cash and waited for her to return with her change. Zyrian's phone rung and he excused himself from the table, right as Angel was making her way back over to them.

"This is my pops. I'll meet you out front," Zyrian said right before he walked outside with his phone up to his ear.

"Here you go Rylee," Angel said as she handed her the receipt and her change.

"Thanks Angel. So, how long have you been working here?" Rylee pried.

"Not that long. It's been a little over two weeks now," she replied.

"Well, it's a good thing that you left MJ's anyway. I'm not sure what's going to happen with it once me and Mekhi get divorced."

"Divorced!" Angel yelled, causing other people to look over at them.

"Yeah, shocking, right?" Rylee giggled.

"Not really. He's the reason why I left MJ's in the first place," Angel said, making Rylee look at her sideways.

"And why is that?" Rylee asked, even though she kind of figured what the answer would be.

"I'm so sorry Rylee. I never meant for things to turn out the way that they did. I met Mekhi before I even started working at the bar and before I even knew you. We messed around for a while and it was all good until I ended up pregnant."

"Pregnant!" Rylee repeated as her heart plummeted in her chest. "You were pregnant by Mekhi?"

"Yes, but he went crazy when he found out. He begged me to get an abortion, and I did. I was in a bad place in my life at the time. I was about to be evicted from my apartment and I threatened to tell you if Mekhi didn't help me out financially. That's how I ended up working at MJ's. He refused to give me any money, but he told me that I could work for it. Needless to say, he meant that in more ways than one."

"So, that's what the attitudes were all about. You were fucking my husband and you got mad at me for whatever reason," Rylee said, as more of a statement rather than a question.

"I apologize Rylee. You were always nice to me and I shouldn't have come at you like I did. I was wrong and I had no reason to be upset with you. I can't even be mad with Mekhi. He told me what it was, but I chose to stay and put up with it. You came first and I knew that from day one," Angel admitted.

She swore that she would never tell Rylee what went down between her and Mekhi, but she was happy that she did. A huge burden had been lifted from her shoulders and she was happy to finally be coming clean. Mekhi had been getting away with his wrong doings for too long and it was time that he was stopped. She wasn't trying to downplay her role in the situation because she was as much to blame as he was.

"Wow," was all that Rylee managed to say once Angel finished talking.

"Again Rylee, I apologize for the part that I played in everything," Angel said sincerely.

"Your apologies aren't necessary or needed at this point. The damage is already done. I'm sure that if Mekhi was still dicking you down on the regular, you wouldn't even be standing here pouring your heart out to me right now. He played you and you feel stupid. That's the only reason why you're confessing. You're salty and it shows. But, I thank you for the info. You just helped me to see that I've made the right decision. Here, you can keep the change. It looks like you can use it," Rylee said as she tossed a few

160 | P a g e

crumpled-up bills on the table and walked out, leaving Angel speechless.

Rylee walked outside and found Zyrian leaning up against her car, still talking on his phone. Once he saw Rylee walking over to him, he ended the call with his father and got into the car. Zyrian was secretly hoping that his sister wasn't home because he wanted to spend some more time with Rylee. She didn't know it, but he was studying everything about her. He paid attention to her likes, dislikes, and everything in between. He noticed how simple things meant so much to her. Just spending time with her family made her smile and Zyrian liked that.

"I guess Zyra is still out having fun," Rylee said when they pulled up in the driveway.

Zyrian was happy that his sister wasn't home and he hoped that she didn't rush getting there.

"Yep, it looks like it's just me and you again." He smiled.

"Zyrian, I appreciate you wanting to be here for me, but you need to get out of this house. I'll be okay," Rylee promised him.

"I'm good, I don't have nothing to do."

"Stop lying. That phone has been ringing off the hook all day. I know a lot of women are mad with me for stealing their time. Especially that tall one with the bad weave," Rylee said, taking a cheap shot at Renata.

"Don't tell me you're jealous. What were you looking at her weave for?" Zyrian asked.

"I'm not jealous at all. And I wasn't looking at her weave, her weave was looking at me. I'm used to seeing the train on the tracks, but hers derailed," Rylee said, making him laugh.

"Girl, shut up and get out of the car," Zyrian chuckled.

He and Rylee sat around and watched movies for over three hours before she decided to call it a night. While she was upstairs taking a shower, Zyrian returned a few phone calls and text messages from earlier. Renata was asking when she would be seeing him again, since it had been over two weeks since they'd last seen each other. He'd been so busy hanging with Rylee that everybody else faded into the background. Renata was cool though, so he made a promise to spend some time with her soon. About an hour later, Zyrian noticed that his phone was going dead and needed to be charged. He thought that Rylee would come back down, but she must have gone straight to bed. It was well after midnight, so he was getting ready to shower and turn in as well. He bypassed the room that Rylee occupied and went to the bathroom down the hall.

Twenty minutes later, Zyrian was done and ready to call it a night. On his way to his room, he passed by Rylee's room again, but it wasn't as quiet as it was before. He heard sniffling and immediately knew that Rylee must have been crying. Most likely, her circumstances really hit her at night, and Zyrian understood how she felt. When he was locked up, the nights were the hardest for him to get through for a while. That's when most of the problems that people ran from during the day came back to haunt them. For Zyrian, that's when the nightmares from his childhood returned full force.

"Don't even lie and say that you're alright because I know you're not," Zyrian said as he climbed into the bed and pulled Rylee into him from behind. She melted in his embrace and tried her best to stop the tears from flowing. She was embarrassed that Zyrian even had to witness it. It had been almost a month and things didn't seem to be getting any better. It didn't help that she kept getting hit with more bullshit about Mekhi every day.

"You remember the girl at the restaurant that came up and spoke to me?" Rylee questioned.

"Yeah," Zyrian answered in his deep baritone voice.

"Well, she just informed me that she was fucking Mekhi too. And not only that, she claimed that she was pregnant by him, but she had an abortion."

"Seriously?" Zyrian asked.

"Yep, he was really playing me for a fool. My whole damn marriage was a lie. I swear, I hate his ass," Rylee replied angrily.

"Give it time baby girl. One day, you'll wake up and this shit won't even bother you anymore."

"I know and I hope that day comes soon. But, in the meantime, I think I need to get tested," Rylee mumbled.

"Tested? You think you're pregnant or something?" Zyrian questioned.

"No, I know I'm not pregnant. I'm talking about being tested for STD's. That bastard was out there having unprotected sex and them coming home to me. The count is three so far, but there's no telling how many other women he's been with."

"I think that's a good idea. We can make an appointment to do it next week," Zyrian said.

"Who is we?" Rylee asked.

"We as in me and you. I can't have my wifey stressing out about nothing like this," Zyrian said, making her blush in the darkness.

"Sounds like somebody is still crushing on me," Rylee smirked.

"Definitely. Probably even more now," he admitted.

"But you don't say it anymore like you used to."

"Because I don't want to be your rebound Rylee. Honestly, you're not even sure about what you want to do yet. You and dude were together for a minute, so I know that your feelings won't just go away. I can't put myself in a position to get hurt. I'm patient, so I don't mind waiting it out. I can't say that I'll wait forever, but we'll see how it goes," Zyrian replied honestly.

"I understand what you're saying, but my mind is made up. I want a divorce."

"Okay, but have you even started the process?" Zyrian asked, even though he already knew the answer.

"No," Rylee answered in a small voice.

"That's my point. You're still undecided and that's okay. That's not a decision that you can make overnight. But stop making excuses for why you haven't done it yet. It's not about the clothes that you left there, like you're trying to make yourself believe. You're conflicted and you should be. This is a life changing decision that shouldn't be rushed."

"Damn, why couldn't I have met and married you first," Rylee snickered.

"It's not the way it was written." Zyrian shrugged. "Go to sleep. I'll stay here until you do."

Rylee smiled, even though he couldn't see her in the darkness. Even though Zyrian probably wasn't trying, he was winning her over every time he opened his mouth. It's like he always knew what to say and when to say it. Rylee didn't want to jump into anything else so soon, but she could see herself being with Zyrian. Maybe it was the loneliness talking, but only time would tell.

Chapter 17

Rylee was heated, as she and Amber sat in the kitchen at their grandmother's house. She'd just come back from her and Mekhi's house trying to get some more of her belongings, and he'd changed the code to the security system. Rylee entered in every possible number combination that she could think of, and nothing worked. When the house phone started ringing, she already knew that the alarm company was calling for verification. Instead of answering the phone, she and Amber hurriedly left before the police came out. Rylee knew that they were probably on the way, since no one had answered the phone. She wanted to stay until the police came, but her cousin wasn't having it.

"Now what?" Amber questioned. "He gets to keep your stuff just because y'all aren't together?"

"Hell no, he's not keeping my shit. I have to ask Mr. Campbell what I can do about that. He hooked me up with a divorce lawyer, but he's not doing anything. He hasn't even drawn up the papers to serve Mekhi yet. Over two months and he ain't did a damn thing," Rylee fumed.

"What's going to happen with MJ's?" Amber asked.

"Fuck MJ's! They can close that bitch down for all I care!" Rylee yelled, right as her grandmother entered the kitchen.

"You watch your mouth Rylee Ann!" Sara yelled at her.

"Sorry grandma," Rylee mumbled.

"That low down son of a bitch is going to get what's

coming to him, so don't you worry about that," Sara fussed.

"Grandma!" Amber yelled. "I can't believe you're using that kind of language."

"Shut up Amber. I'm pissed and I can say whatever I feel like saying. Messing with my grandbabies is like messing with me. I can't believe that low down dirty dog," Sara fumed.

"But you just fussed at me for cursing and you're doing the same thing," Rylee laughed.

"You shut up too, Rylee. Once you get to be my age, you can do whatever you want to do. You give me that lawyer's number and I'll call him myself. I want you divorced from that bastard as soon as possible. Oh, Lord, help me. I'll be praying all night if I keep up with this mouth of mine," Sara remarked.

Rylee and Amber continued laughing as she walked away, still mumbling obscenities under her breath. When Rylee's phone started ringing, she jumped up from the table and walked out the front door. Mekhi was calling her back and she didn't want her grandmother to hear her cursing him out. She'd been calling him all morning, trying to get the code to the security system and he was just now returning her call.

"What kind of fucking games are you playing Mekhi? Why would you change the security code and not tell me?" Rylee yelled when she answered the phone.

"I'm not the one that's playing games. Why were you trying to move your shit out while I'm not home? I've been begging you to talk to me for weeks, but you blocked my number out instead. The only reason why you unblocked me at all is because my call is benefiting you," Mekhi responded.

"I'm not understanding what we have to talk about. I just need my stuff out of your house and that's the only conversation that I want to have with you."

"So, it's my house now?" Mekhi questioned.

"It is until the judge makes a decision on what we should do with it," Rylee answered.

"You know damn well I'm not giving you a divorce Rylee. You can get that shit out of your head. You keep throwing it in my face that I cheated, but you ain't no better. You don't think people tell me how much you and that nigga Zyrian be together? I already knew that y'all been had something going on. That's probably why you want a divorce so bad. You letting that nigga get in your head."

"You sound stupid. Just let me come get the rest of my shit and you won't have to worry about hearing from me again," Rylee promised.

"Answer this for me, Rylee. You claimed to be scared to death when I wanted you to ride on my bike with me. What's so special about Zyrian that you would hop on the back of his bike?"

"Nigga, you barely know how to ride the damn bike yourself. I would have been a damn fool to let you kill me. You sound like a bitter bitch, worrying about the next man. All of this extra conversation is unnecessary. When can I come get the rest of my stuff? I don't even care if you're home or not. I'm tired of buying stuff when I already have everything I need."

"How many times do I have to apologize to you, Rylee? Baby, I swear I've learned my lesson. We can go to marriage counseling or whatever you want to do. I just don't want our marriage to end. I love you and I'm sorry," Mekhi whined pathetically.

"Exactly what are you sorry about Mekhi? Are you sorry about the picture that was sent to your phone? Or is fucking Brandy the reason? No, maybe you're sorry about fucking Angel and getting her pregnant. Exactly what are you sorry for?" Rylee asked sarcastically.

Mekhi was speechless. He couldn't believe that Rylee knew about Angel. That, among other things, was something that he never wanted her to find out. Things were not going like he wanted them to go and he was getting more depressed by the day.

"Baby-" Mekhi started.

"Don't baby me," Rylee said, cutting him off. "Just tell me when I can come get the rest of my shit."

"We'll talk about it whenever you're ready to sit down and have an adult conversation about our marriage," Mekhi said right before he hung up the phone.

"Stupid ass!" Rylee yelled before tossing her phone in the passenger's seat.

Mekhi was starting something, but Rylee was determined to finish it. There was no way in hell that she was going back to his lying, cheating ass. He was going to regret the day that he cheated on her, and Rylee was going to make sure of that. She called Amber's phone and told her that she was leaving and would talk to her later. Mekhi had ruined her mood and she was ready to go back to Zyra's house and chill.

As soon as she pulled up to the house, she frowned at yet another annoyance. Renata's car was parked right next to Zyrian's, making Rylee frown up in disgust. Renata was cool, but Rylee hated the way that she always all over Zyrian. She had to be touching him or running her hand through his waves, and it made Rylee sick.

"Hey y'all," Rylee said when she walked through the door.

Zyrian had his head in Renata's lap, but he quickly sat upright when Rylee came in. It was crazy, but he didn't feel right being with another woman when she was around. Zyrian noticed that Rylee rolled her eyes, right before she went to sit next to Zyra. He wasn't sure what that was all about, but he would definitely ask her later. He was ready for Renata to go since Rylee was home, but he didn't want to be rude.

"What happened?" Zyra asked her friend.

"That bastard changed the security code to the alarm system. I would have stayed and got my shit, but Amber's scary ass started panicking."

"Girl, Amber is crazy. You know she's scared of her own shadow," Zyra laughed.

"I don't know what made me bring her nervous ass with me in the first place. I'm going to call Mr. Campbell and see what's taking his lawyer friend so long to handle his business," Rylee fussed as she got up and headed for the stairs.

Zyrian wanted to go talk to her, but he couldn't leave his guest downstairs while he did. Suddenly, he had regrets about allowing Renata to come over. She didn't do anything wrong, but she wasn't who he wanted to be with. He thought that Rylee would be gone for a while, but she came back sooner than he thought.

"You okay?" Renata asked when she saw Zyrian move away from her and lie down on the other end of the sofa.

"Yeah, I'm just tired." Zyrian fake yawned, hoping that she would take the bait.

"Oh, well, let me get going so you can get you some rest," Renata said, buying right into the game that he was playing.

Zyrian got up and walked her to her car and watched as she pulled off. As soon as she was out of sight, he ran back inside and right into Zyra.

"You fake as hell for that. Since when do you go to bed this early," Zyra laughed.

"Mind your business girl. I'm going to see what's up with my baby," Zyrian replied.

"You better not be trying to play with my friend's feelings Zyrian. You know what she just went through."

"No, your friend better not play with my feelings. I already feel like I'm in too deep and her ass is still married," Zyrian said as he walked away to Rylee's bedroom.

Rylee was on the phone when he walked into the bedroom, so he sat down right next to her. He could tell that she was talking to an attorney because she was writing down a case number and some dates on the notepad in her hand. She seemed to be deep into the conversation, so Zyrian played on his phone and waited until she was done.

"What's up?" Rylee asked once she was finished with her call.

"I should be asking you that. You came in here rolling your eyes and shit like I did you something," Zyrian replied.

"I didn't roll my eyes at you," Rylee denied.

"So, you lying to me now?" Zyrian asked.

"Why are you even up here? Don't you have company?"

"Were you mad that I had company?" Zyrian asked while looking directly into her eyes.

"Honestly, yes," Rylee said truthfully while staring right back at him.

Zyrian nodded his head in understanding. He loved Rylee's honesty, but she really didn't have a reason to be jealous. She was who he wanted. The timing was just off. Zyrian got up to turn on the night lite that was plugged up on the side of the bed. Once that was on, he turned off the big light and kneeled in front of Rylee. He removed her shoes from her feet, before removing his own and climbing into bed with her in a spooning position. This had become a nightly routine for them and they both looked forward to it.

"You know I got you if you need something Rylee. If that nigga don't want to give you your clothes, I'll buy you some more," Zyrian offered.

"I appreciate you, Zyrian, but I can buy my own clothes. It's crazy that I should have to do that when I have a huge wardrobe at the house. I'm just ready for all of this to be over with. Now, I'm finding out that the lawyer has been trying to have him served, but he can't catch up with him. He's doing that shit on purpose," Rylee argued.

"That nigga know what he's doing. He doesn't want a divorce and he's trying to avoid it. I understand that you want your stuff from the house, but just know that I got you if you need me."

"I know you do Zyrian. That means a lot to me." Rylee smiled.

"Yeah, even though you let that nigga make you stop coming over here."

"I wish you would stop saying that. I didn't stop coming over here. I just came over when you were gone. I wasn't trying to commit adultery."

"That's why you're my wifey. You know more about loyalty than most of these niggas out here," Zyrian acknowledged.

"So, how do you feel? Zyra said that you didn't sleep too good last night. I know that yesterday was your friend's birthday. Are you okay?" Rylee asked as she turned her body to face him. She felt Zyrian tense up, but he relaxed after a few seconds.

"I'm good," he said, hoping that would be the end of the conversation.

"Do you wanna talk about it?" Rylee asked.

Aside from Zyra telling her that Zyrian almost died in a bad car accident when he was younger, she didn't know much about the story. Rylee wasn't satisfied with his short answer and she wanted to know everything that happened. Zyrian hated talking about his childhood accident, but he decided to get it over with and tell her the entire truth.

"Listen, I'll tell you what happened, but let this be the end of it. I hate reliving the past, but I know you won't be satisfied until I tell you every detail," Zyrian sighed.

"Ok, I'm listening," Rylee said as she sat up and grabbed both of his hands.

Zyrian sighed loudly before he started. "When I was thirteen, my best friend Darius and his family invited me to go with them to Disney World. He was an only child, so we spent a lot of time together. We packed up their Tahoe and prepared to make the almost ten-hour drive to stay there for a week. After a few hours, Darius and I got tired. I got on the third-row seat to go to sleep and left him on the first row. After that, the only thing I remember is Darius' mother screaming and me flying out of the back window. I woke up two days later in the hospital to find out that I was the only one who had survived the crash. I had two broken legs, as well as a bunch of other injuries. A construction truck driver fell asleep behind the wheel of his truck and crashed right into us. They said that me flying out of the back window is probably what saved my life."

"Oh, my God, Zyrian," Rylee gasped when he finished telling his story.

"Yeah and the crazy part about it is the driver walked away untouched. Not even a scratch on his body and he caused the accident."

"Did he get charged or go to jail?" Rylee asked.

"Yeah, but he didn't do that much time. He killed three people and got a fucking slap on the wrist." Zyrian frowned.

"Why didn't your parents sue? He was at fault and his company should have paid."

"We did sue them bastards. Twenty million dollars is what my best friend and his parents were worth to them. I got ten million and Darius' grandmother got the other ten, since she was the next of kin. Sad part is I barely even put a dent in my portion. Aside from buying my shop and me and my parents' houses, it's just sitting up in the bank collecting interest. I feel guilty every time I even think about touching it," Zyrian confessed.

"But, you don't have anything to feel guilty about Zyrian. You didn't cause the accident. You were a victim, just like the rest of them," Rylee reasoned.

"Buck always tells me the same thing, but I just can't shake that feeling. I know it sounds crazy, but it is what it is. That's why I keep telling you that I got you if you need anything. Even if it's another house," Zyrian said seriously.

"Thanks, Zyrian, but I could never ask you to do something like that," Rylee refused. "I might not have nearly as much as you have in the bank, but I'm comfortable. Once this divorce is finalized, I'll get another house and another business to run as well."

"You didn't ask, I offered. Besides, it's not like I can't afford it." Zyrian shrugged.

"I would have never known if you wouldn't have said anything. That couldn't be Mekhi sitting on all those millions. Everybody and their mama would know with his bragging ass. I love your modesty," Rylee said.

"Mekhi ain't used to nothing. A nigga who really got it is probably the most silent one in the room. The loudest person is usually the weakest," Zyrian maintained.

"Well, I guess I married a weak nigga," Rylee acknowledged.

"It's cool though. You gon' be getting with a real nigga sooner than you think," Zyrian replied.

He and Rylee stared into each other's eyes for a while, before she moved her body forward until their lips were inches apart.

"Nope," Zyrian smirked before Rylee's lip could touch his.

"What do you mean no? What's so different now? When I was married, you were all on me. Now, you act like it's a crime to even touch me." Rylee frowned.

"Correction, you're still married and it's very different now. At first, it was just about hitting it. Now that my feelings are involved, I'm not going there with you until I'm convinced that you and ole boy are done for good," Zyrian informed her.

"We are done for good," Rylee swore.

"That's what your mouth says, but I'll be the judge of that. Go do what I'm about to do and take you a cold shower," Zyrian laughed as he got up from the bed and walked out of the room.

"Bastard!" Rylee yelled while throwing a pillow at him.

As bad as she wanted to kiss him, Rylee understood what he was saying. Although she was sure about her status with Mekhi, Zyrian was still skeptical. He was resisting her now, but he wouldn't be able to turn her down forever. Rylee was patient, so she didn't mind waiting.

Chapter 18

"**A**nswer the phone, you miserable bitch. I know you see me calling. You better not let me catch your hating ass on the streets," Mekhi slurred into the phone.

He'd been calling Angel's phone non-stop, leaving all kinds of threatening messages, but she never answered for him. Mekhi was pissed when Rylee mentioned him getting Angel pregnant. He kept wondering when did they see each other and how did the conversation become about him. Angel claimed that she wasn't bitter, but her actions showed otherwise. Mekhi didn't want her anymore and she couldn't handle it. Then, there was Shay. She was back to dropping Mekhya off at his mother's house whenever she felt like it. Mekhi had been going through so much with Rylee that he hadn't paid the daycare or child support in two months. That was the last thing on his mind and he really didn't care how Shay felt. She kept threatening to take him back to court, but he was unbothered. She caught him slipping the last time, but he didn't plan to let that happen again.

"You about ready for me to lock up Mr. Jameson?" his manager, Frank, asked for the second time.

"I'll lock up. You can leave Frank," Mekhi answered.

"Are you sure? I don't think it'll be a good idea to leave you here by yourself. You can't drive home in your condition," Frank observed.

"I said leave!" Mekhi yelled angrily, as he continued to gulp down the liquor from the bottle that sat in front of him.

Frank nodded his head, but he knew that leaving was not an option. He walked over to Mekhi's office and looked through the rolodex that was on his desk. He knew that Mekhi and Rylee had been separated for a few months, but he needed to call somebody there to get him. Frank's wife had been outside waiting to pick him up for over twenty minutes and he was ready to go. Mekhi's mother's number was the first one that he came across and he wasted no time making the call.

"Hi, this is Frank and I'm one of the manager and MJ's. I'm calling for Mekhi Jameson's mother," Frank said when a woman answered the phone.

"This is his sister, Mena. Is something wrong with my brother?" she asked in a panicked tone.

"No, nothing is wrong, but I was wondering if somebody could come and pick him up. He's been drinking a lot and I don't want to let him drive himself home," Frank answered.

"Oh, well, I don't have a car, but I'll get my brother Kendrick to pick him up. We don't live too far, so he won't be long. Just wait with him until he gets there."

"Okay, thanks," Frank sighed before hanging up.

This was one of the reasons why he was looking for another job. Mekhi was alright in the beginning, but Frank was starting to hate him with a passion. Mekhi didn't know how to talk to his employees and he had no problems letting everybody know that he was running shit. Frank wasn't about to let someone younger than him speak to him any kind of way. On the low, he was happy that Rylee left Mekhi. He was always flirting with the women who came there, but he acted as if he was the picture-perfect husband whenever Rylee was around. Most likely, she found out about some of his wrong doings and hit the highway. Not that Frank felt sorry for him. Anything that happened was just what his no-good ass deserved. About ten minutes later, Frank heard the front door buzzer going off. He rushed to disarm the alarm and let who he assumed was Mekhi's brother come in.

"Where that stupid ass nigga at?" Kendrick asked as he walked into the building.

"He's still sitting at the bar," Frank replied while leading the way.

"Ole dumb ass. Rylee left and that nigga is going down the drain. That's what he gets for always trying to talk down on everybody else," Kendrick remarked.

Although Frank agreed with everything that he'd just said, he decided not to comment. No matter how he felt about the situation, Mekhi and Kendrick were still brothers. He refused to get thrown into the middle of their sibling rivalry.

"His car is out back but, if he needs a ride tomorrow, tell him to call me," Frank offered.

"Come on bruh!" Kendrick yelled as he roughly tapped on Mekhi's shoulder.

Instead of standing to his feet, Mekhi slumped over in his chair and almost fell.

"Whoa!" Frank shouted as he and Kendrick helped him up.

"Help me take him to my car," Kendrick ordered as threw his brother's limp arm over his shoulder.

Both men carried a drunken Mekhi out to the car and helped him get in. Kendrick waited around until Frank locked up before they pulled off, going in different directions. It took Kendrick about another fifteen minutes to get to Mekhi's house. Once he pulled into the driveway, he walked around the car and opened the door for his brother.

"I gotta throw up," Mekhi announced as soon as Kendrick helped him out.

"Shit! Your ass needs to stop drinking if you can't handle your liquor!" Kendrick yelled, right as Mekhi heaved the contents of his stomach onto the pavement, narrowly missing his feet.

Kendrick guided his younger brother to the front door of the house and fished around in his pocket for his keys. Once he had them in his hands, he tried a few of them until he found the right one. Kendrick opened the door and almost dropped Mekhi on the marble tiled floors when the alarm started blaring loudly.

"Damn, Mekhi, get up nigga. What's the code to the alarm system?" Kendrick inquired while shaking him.

"It's um...." Mekhi replied while dry heaving like he wanted to throw up again.

"It's what nigga? I need to turn this shit off before the police be coming here!" Kendrick yelled.

"My wallet," Mekhi mumbled groggily.

Kendrick rushed him over to the sofa and sat him down. He reached into his back pocket and grabbed his wallet, right as the phone started to ring. After flipping through a pile of credit cards and other business cards, Kendrick finally located a card for the alarm company with the code written on the back of it.

"Stupid ass nigga," Kendrick remarked after disarming the system.

Mekhi was even dumber than he'd previously assumed. Anybody could have stolen his wallet and had access to his home as well. Once the alarm was no longer roaring, Kendrick answered his brother's ringing phone and gave the operator the password that was scribbled on the back of the card. He was finally able to exhale once the door was locked and there was no threat of the police showing up. Kendrick took the opportunity to look around the house to see how his brother was really living. He and his brother weren't the best of friends, so that was only his third time being in his house. Mekhi and Rylee were doing the damn thing and their house was solid proof of that. They had it decorated nicely and everything that they owned looked expensive. Kendrick wandered into their bedroom and opened the door to a huge walk-in closet. It must have been Rylee's because everything inside belonged to a female. He walked out and opened another door and walked into Mekhi's personal space. He nodded his head in approval as he thumbed through some of designer clothes that his brother often bragged about.

Seeing how his younger brother was living made Kendrick want to step his game up. He could see himself living in a nice house and wearing designer clothes too. After feeling like he'd pried long enough, Kendrick went back into the living room and sat on the sofa opposite of the one that Mekhi was on. He turned on the tv and got comfortable, preparing to stay the night. Although Mekhi got on his nerves at times, that was still his little brother and he didn't want to see anything happen to him. While flipping through channels trying to find something to watch, Kendrick got up to see who kept calling one of his brother's phones.

"Hello," Kendrick answered the restricted number that appeared on the screen.

"Mekhi?" a woman questioned on the other end of the line.

"No, this is Kendrick. Who is this?"

The line went dead and Kendrick looked at the screen to see that the woman had hung up on him. Her voice sounded familiar, but he wasn't sure about who it was. Before putting his phone down again, Kendrick decided to pry a little bit further and looked at his brother's text messages. Seeing that the phone was practically empty, Kendrick put it down, right as a text message came through on the other phone. When he saw that it was from Rylee, he opened the message and laughed out loud. Rylee was always popping off about one thing or another and she was going in on Mekhi about everything under the sun. Aside from her calling him a cheating dog, she was going off about Mekhi not giving her the new code to the alarm system. She kept saying that she wanted the rest of her clothes and that she couldn't wait to be divorced from him.

Mekhi had been tight lipped about his split with Rylee, but he wasn't surprised to know that he'd got caught cheating. He scrolled through a few more and saw messages from Shay, practically begging him to pay their daughter's daycare bill. Mekhi was the most pathetic father that he'd ever seen, but no one could tell Carolyn that. Kendrick put the phone down and shook his head. After returning to his spot on the sofa, Kendrick watched a movie until he drifted off to sleep.

*****

Mekhi woke up the next morning to a terrible headache. He tried sitting up too fast and the stinging pain in his head knocked him back down. Due to the blackout curtains surrounding the windows in his house, he couldn't tell if it was daylight or not. Once he calmed down for a few minutes, he focused on the cable box and saw that it was after one in the afternoon. After slowly sitting up, Mekhi looked on the table in front of him and saw his blowfish hangover medicine and a bottle of water. He hurriedly gulped a few pills down with the water and sat back with his arm partially covering his face. Mekhi's eyes popped open at the realization that he wasn't at home alone. The last thing he remembered from the night before was sitting at the bar at MJ's trying to drink his problems away.

Just as he was reminiscing about the night before, the scent of food being cooked invaded his nostrils. Mekhi was hit with a wave of nausea and raced to the bathroom, right before he regurgitated the lining of his stomach into the toilet. After brushing his teeth, Mekhi rushed through the house to see who was making themselves at home in his kitchen. He wished to the heavens above that it was his wife, but he got instantly heated when he saw Kendrick standing at his stove instead.

"What the fuck are you doing in my house?" Mekhi bellowed through the constant banging in his head.

"Well, hello to you too," Kendrick piped sarcastically.

"This ain't the time for you to be playing with me, bruh. What are you doing here and how did you get in? You in my kitchen cooking and shit like you live here," Mekhi argued.

"Nigga, I helped you out. You were drunk out of your mind and couldn't drive home. I picked you up from MJ's and stayed here to make sure you were straight. This is the thanks I get for coming to your rescue?" Kendrick questioned.

"I'm thankful and I'm straight. You can bounce now," Mekhi replied while snatching the spatula from his hand.

"Man, fuck you Mekhi, bruh, straight up. That's why Rylee left your stupid ass now. You think the sun rise and set on your arrogant ass. Next time, mama gon' be burying you because I ain't doing shit for you no more," Kendrick swore.

"You never did do shit for me. Fuck you mean? Nigga, I got money and lots of it."

"Yeah, okay, keep talking that hot shit. That's just how it's gon' happen to you. And find somebody else to bring you to pick up your car from MJ's," Kendrick said as he picked up his keys and headed for the front of the house.

"Penniless bastard," Mekhi scoffed once Kendrick slammed the door.

He locked up behind him and headed straight for the shower. Mekhi was thankful that his brother got him home safely, but he didn't want his broke ass thinking that he could hang around his house all day. It was bad enough that he was there without his knowledge in the first place.

Chapter 19

❝ It's almost three now, so how does four o'clock sound?" Mekhi asked happily.

He was excited and he couldn't hide it if he tried. After three months of separation, he and Rylee were finally meeting up to have a much-needed discussion. The best part about everything was that Rylee was the one who initiated the meeting. She was tired of them being at each other's throats and Mekhi couldn't agree more.

"That's fine, I'll be there," Rylee replied.

"Okay baby, I love you," Mekhi said.

"I love you too," Rylee replied before she hung up the phone.

Zyra sat next to her, snickering the entire time that she was talking.

"Shut up Zyra. I'm surprised he didn't hear your dumb ass in here laughing," Rylee fussed.

"I'm sorry girl, but I couldn't help it. I can't believe that he fell for that stupid shit after y'all been separated for three whole months."

"Fuck him. Let me call my lawyer and tell him where he's going to be, so he can go serve him his papers," Rylee announced as she dialed the number on her phone.

Rylee's lawyer, Mr. Givens, had decided that sending a sheriff to serve Mekhi was not a good idea. He decided to use a court appointed curator instead. That way, Mekhi would never see the person coming when the time came. Mekhi was smart, so Rylee and her lawyer had to be smarter.

"You better be happy that Zyrian wasn't here. He would have been pissed hearing you say you love another man," Zyra laughed once Rylee was off the phone.

"That's why I didn't tell him what was going on. I don't need him trying to discourage me," Rylee answered.

Rylee and Zyrian were only friends, but she knew that it would eventually turn into more. They both wanted more, but the timing just wasn't right. He wasn't trying to go there with her until he was sure that she was done with Mekhi for good, and she had to respect that. They'd been sleeping in the same bed for the past two weeks but hadn't shared so much as a kiss on the cheek. Rylee knew that he still talked to other females all the time, but he never invited them to the house like he used to. That included Renata. She hadn't been over since the last time Rylee walked in and saw his head in her lap. A few times, he would leave the house for a few hours and Rylee was sure that was his time to hook up with some female companionship.

"You know he would never try to discourage you from getting divorced. He wants that more than anything," Zyra said, shaking her from her thoughts.

"Well, his wish is about to come true," Rylee replied, right as a text message came through her phone from an unknown number.

"What does it say?" Zyra asked when she saw the perplexed look on Rylee's face.

"Somebody just sent me the security code and password to Mekhi's house," Rylee said in shock.

"How do you know that's what it is?" Zyra inquired.

"It's says if you want your shit, go get it. Then, it has a password and some numbers. What else could it be?" Rylee wondered.

"He must have pissed somebody off, but that's a good thing for you. That's perfect Rylee. While he's waiting for you at the restaurant, we can go to the house and get your stuff," Zyra suggested.

"We'll need some help though Zyra. That's a lot of stuff. I'm not leaving anything behind like I did before. I want all of my shit, so I can be done with him."

"We can get Buck and the rest of them to help us," Zyra concluded.

"Hell no, they'll tell Zyrian and I don't want him coming."

"I can call Snake. He won't tell Zyrian and he can get his girlfriend's brothers to help him. Two of them have trucks."

"Okay, let's do it. Let me call Amber and see if she can come help us," Rylee replied.

She was excited that things were looking up for her, as far as getting away from Mekhi. She would have all her belongings out of his house and he was being served with divorce papers. That was all she ever wanted anyway. She hoped that he didn't try to make a big deal out of it but, knowing him, he probably would. As far as the houses and business that they co-owned, Rylee wanted no parts of it. He could have it all, and she would start over from the bottom, just as long as she no longer had the Jameson last name.

"Snake is on his way over. Let's get some garbage bags, so we can fill them up with as much as we can!" Zyra yelled from the hallway.

"Okay, Amber is on her way too. I'm about to change into something comfortable," Rylee said as she ran around the room taking her clothes off.

She threw on a pair of joggers and pulled her hair up in to a high ponytail. After lacing up her Nikes and pulling a t-shirt over her head, Rylee met Zyra in the front room and waited for everybody to get there. Amber was the first to arrive about fifteen minutes later, and Snake and his crew weren't too far behind. It was three-thirty, so Rylee sent Mekhi a text telling him that she was on her way. When he replied telling her that he had just pulled up in Deanie's parking lot, that was music to her ears.

"Let's go; he's already at the restaurant!" Rylee yelled excitedly.

"Aye Rylee, if you want me to make you a rich widow, all you have to do is say the word," Snake offered sincerely.

It always baffled Rylee how he offered to kill people like he was offering a bottle of water. It rolled off his tongue naturally and he didn't even blink an eye when he said it. Zyra was used to him talking like that, but Rylee never knew how to respond to such an offer.

"Uh, thanks Snake, but I don't think that will be necessary. I just need my stuff from the house and I'll be good after that." Rylee smiled through her nervousness.

"Alright, but just know that the offer is always there. You're family now," Snake replied.

Rylee nodded in response as they all walked out of the house. She got into the car with Amber, while Zyra took her own car. Snake rode in his truck with one man, while two other men followed behind them in another truck. Rylee had clothes and shoes for days, and she needed all the help that she could get. Traffic was light so, ten minutes later, they were pulling up to house.

"You need me to get out Rylee?" Amber asked anxiously.

"I need help carrying everything out, but I understand if you want to stay in the car Amber. I'll try to do this as quickly as possible," Rylee promised.

"No, I'm coming," Amber offered.

"I won't be upset if you don't want to Amber. I understand."

"You would do it for me, so I'm doing it for you. Let's go," Amber said, surprising her cousin.

Everyone followed Rylee up to the front door and waited until she unlocked it. When the alarm went off, Rylee prayed that the anonymous text that she received was accurate. Suddenly, she felt foolish for jumping up and just going over there without knowing for sure. Putting the negative thoughts to the side, Rylee entered the number that she had into the key pad. She released the nervous breath that she'd been holding once the system granted her access into the home.

"Okay, this is my closet and I need everything out of it," Rylee instructed the men who had accompanied her there.

She didn't have to tell them twice. They started grabbing all her clothes that were on hangers and bringing them outside to the awaiting vehicles. Zyra and Amber started grabbing shoes, while Rylee grabbed her underclothes and toiletries. She was happy to see that Snake and his crew were moving like lightning and almost half of her closet was empty already. When Rylee's phone alerted her of a text message, she stopped momentarily to see who it was. When she saw that it was Mekhi, Rylee's heart dropped until she read what he was saying. It was a little after four and he wanted to know if she was having trouble parking. Rylee lied and said that she was stuck in a little traffic, and he assured her that he didn't mind waiting.

"Is that him?" Zyra asked.

"Yeah, I told him that I was in traffic, so he's cool," Rylee answered.

"We're almost done anyway. Ten more minutes and we should be out of here. You might have to put some of this stuff in one of the empty bedrooms. I didn't know you had this much shit," Zyra laughed.

"I told her that she has a shopping addiction, but she didn't believe me." Amber smiled.

They continued to work until everything that Rylee owned was packed up into the four cars that they had come in. Rylee smiled, just imagining the look on Mekhi's face when he came home and saw that her closet and all her drawers were empty.

"Well, we did what we came to do. You ready honey?" Zyra asked Rylee.

"Yes. I feel so much better now that I have all of my stuff." Rylee smiled.

"We'll meet y'all at the house so we can carry everything in," Snake announced, right before he and his boys left.

"Okay, I'm gone too. Lock up and get the hell out of here," Zyra told Rylee while walking to the front door.

"We're coming right behind you," Rylee said, right before Zyra left.

She and Amber double checked the bedroom and bathroom, making sure that they had everything before they left.

"You want something to drink Amber?" Rylee asked her cousin.

"Yeah and then we need to leave. I don't want Mekhi to show up and we're still here. I would have felt better if Snake was still here, but I'm scared now," Amber admitted.

"I'm ready. I got everything that I needed. Here you go," Rylee said, handing her a bottle of water.

It had only been a few months since she left, but Mekhi hadn't changed anything. They didn't have much food in the freezer like they usually did, but that was about the only difference that she noticed.

"Ready?" Rylee asked her cousin.

"Yes," Amber answered as she followed her to the door.

As soon as Rylee opened the door, she jumped, startled by the woman who stood on the other side. She had her had in midair, like she was about to knock or ring the doorbell.

"Shit," Rylee said as she held her chest. "You scared me. Can I help you?"

"Yes, I'm looking for Mekhi," the woman replied with a bit of an attitude.

Rylee ignored her aggressive stance and looked down at who the woman had with her. She was surprised to see her holding the hand of the same little girl that she'd seen at Carolyn's house a few months ago. The same little girl that she was told that Kendrick had fathered.

"Mekhi is not here. What's your name? I'll tell him that you and your daughter came by," Rylee said, trying to get her to reveal who she was and the reason for her visit.

"My name is Shay and you can tell him that me and our daughter, Mekhya, came by to see him," Shay replied with a satisfied smirk.

To Be Continued...

Made in the USA
Monee, IL
04 November 2019